# CREAM PUFF KILLER

## LEXY BAKER COZY MYSTERY SERIES BOOK 13

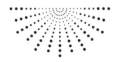

## LEIGHANN DOBBS

LEIGHANN DOBBS PUBLISHING

This is a work of fiction. None of it is real. All names, places, and events are products of the author's imagination. Any resemblance to real names, places, or events are purely coincidental, and should not be construed as being real.

CREAM PUFF KILLER

Copyright © 2017

Leighann Dobbs Publishing

http://www.leighanndobbs.com

*A*sking her grandmother's friend Ruth for a ride to drop off pastries for a client hadn't been one of Lexy Baker-Perillo's brightest ideas. Who knew getting a ride in Ruth's 1970s Oldsmobile would include being stuffed into a cab with four senior citizens just in order to retrieve the darn thing?

Lexy shifted position, trying to get comfortable, which was nearly impossible considering that she was wedged between her grandmother, Mona Baker—or Nans, as Lexy called her—and Nans' friend Ida. As one of four occupants in the backseat of the small cab, she was practically suffocating in the mingled scents of White Shoulders and Chanel No. 5.

To make matters worse, the driver was using fast, jerky maneuvers to navigate the morning traffic, making Lexy wonder if he'd just gotten his driver's license yesterday as she listened to the cream puffs slide around inside the bakery box that rested in her lap. She'd made the cream puffs fresh in her bakery—The Cup and Cake —that morning, and she was trying to deliver them to the Ladies Auxiliary for their luncheon. The Ladies Auxiliary was an important, albeit finicky, client because, if they liked her pastries, they'd spread the word. She could only imagine the damage being done to the once-perfect pastries as they smashed against the side of the box.

"Shouldn't be much longer, ladies," Ruth said cheerily from the front seat of the cab. Easy for *her* to be cheery—she wasn't mashed in like a sardine. Ruth half turned to look back at them. "Everyone comfy?"

"Well, if you don't count the fact I've got an elbow in my ribs," Ida quipped, giving Helen, who sat on the other side of her, a glowering look. "And, Mona, could you scoot a bit more toward your door? Lexy is practically in my lap. Though I wouldn't mind holding that box of pastries." Ida eyed the box, and Lexy could tell she was trying to figure out how to get inside without messing up the perfectly tied bakery twine that held it closed.

"We each have an equal portion of the seat," Nans said, ever the patient leader of their octogenarian group. "It's only a little while longer."

"I just hope my precious Olds survived the winter in good condition." Ruth searched through her enormous beige patent-leather purse. Lexy could only guess for what. Over the years, she'd seen the ladies pull everything from weapons to wet wipes out of their purses. "Poor Nunzio always said she was a cream puff."

"Yes, poor Nunzio, the *crime boss*." Helen gave an imperious sniff, her tone decidedly sarcastic. "I think you're far better off with him joining the dearly departed. Especially considering your narrow brush with the law over his death."

Lexy gave the wary-looking cab driver a small smile. "It's not really what it sounds like. Ruth was eventually cleared of all charges in his murder."

The cab driver gave her a wide-eyed stare then accelerated fast, probably eager to get these crazy broads out of his taxi. Unfortunately, Lexy was used to the reaction by now. She sighed and settled back into her seat and smiled.

Overall, life was good. She and Jack were happily married and enjoying life together in Nans' old house with all of the things Lexy loved from her childhood. Plus, there were new pictures coming in daily from her parents of their exploits on the road. They were traveling the US in an RV, stopping along the way at every attraction that caught their fancy. There'd been the Corn Palace and the World's Biggest Ball of Twine. A few days ago, they'd sent Lexy snapshots from a place called

Peavy's Monster Mart in Arkansas, where her mom and dad had gotten their pictures taken with their heads stuck through a huge painted Sasquatch.

*Fun times.*

Of course, things around her little corner of the world in Brook Ridge Falls were going splendidly too. The ladies were currently living the high life in the local retirement community. At first, when Nans had sold her house to Lexy for only a dollar, Lexy had objected. But now, seeing how happy her grandmother was in her own private condo on the second floor of the retirement community, surrounded by her friends and with activities galore, Lexy realized it had been for the best.

The other ladies' condos were close by, though they often used Nans' as the center of operations. Especially when it came to their amateur sleuthing business, a business that had come in handy more than once for Lexy. The only snag was that Jack didn't always approve of their nosy methods, though even he had to admit the ladies had helped him out on a case a time or two.

The only fly in the ointment for Lexy right now was her beloved VW Bug. The old thing wasn't doing so well. In fact, it had died on her three times recently and was at the shop right now, which was why she had asked Ruth for a ride and, consequently, ended up stuffed into this cab in the first place.

"What's that cute hubby of yours up to today?" Helen piped up from her side of the car.

"Oh, I'm sure he's very busy." Lexy toyed with the pretty pink-and-white twine holding the bakery box closed. That was the other fly in the ointment. Jack had been working a lot more than usual lately. Probably busy with investigations. She shouldn't take it personally, but... "Seems there's always something going on around town."

As a homicide detective in tiny Brook Ridge Falls, New Hampshire, Jack was indeed busy. There always seemed to be some sort of dubious shenanigans happening around town, despite its small size and population, and more often than not, Lexy and Nans and their friends were somehow involved. Much to Jack's chagrin.

She gazed out at the passing scenery, sunshine warming her face and love warming her heart. Marrying Jack had been the best decision of her life, and not just because she was head over heels for the man either. They'd gotten off to an unusual start, having met when Lexy's shih tzu-poodle mix, Sprinkles, had decided that Jack's shrubs were the perfect place for her "business." Of course, the subsequent murder investigation of Lexy's ex, who had eaten a poisoned cupcake from her shop, didn't do much to improve things, especially with Lexy being the prime suspect and Jack the chief investigator. But it had all worked out. Lexy had been cleared, and now they were happily married.

*Funny how the worst situations could end up yielding the most wonderful results...*

Lexy watched as Ruth pulled a pair of white leather racing gloves from her bag. She put them on, waggling her fingers in front of her like an Indy car racer preparing for the 500. The charm bracelet around her wrist jangled merrily.

"You aren't planning to do anything too dangerous, are you?" Lexy asked the older woman, giving her a warning look. According to Nans, Ruth had been a real hellion in her younger days. Dark and exotic and beautiful, like a hothouse lily, she'd drawn the attention of all sorts of men—good and bad alike. Now, at nearly eighty, she still seemed to draw masculine attention like a bug to a zapper, even when it was unwanted.

"Goodness no, dear." Ruth gave her the placid grin of a woman thirty years younger. All the ladies, in fact, looked and acted like women half their age—all spryness and sparkle, and woe to anyone who tried to slow them down. Ruth folded her hands demurely in her lap, belying the spark of mischief in her dark eyes. "I'm just itching to drive. You know I always store the Olds through the winter. Nunzio always said I should take care of it, and he was right. But with spring now upon us, it's time I get her out of storage and rev her engine."

"Hmm," Nans scoffed. "I doubt you have anything to worry about, Lexy, dear. We all know Ruth can barely see over the steering wheel, and her top speed is twenty-five."

"Yep. And that's on the highway." Ida snickered, her wit as sharp as the knives in Lexy's bakery kitchen. She'd always reminded Lexy of a magical imp—short and sweet and always ready for fun, with her lavender-tinged white hair, mischievous blue eyes, and quick steps.

The cab driver turned into the paved parking lot of Stan's Storage, zooming past a long stretch of storage bay buildings on his way toward the automotive section near the back of the large area. Seconds later, they screeched to a halt outside an overhead door, the look on the driver's face a mix of determination and relief. "Here we are, ladies. That will be ten fifty, please."

Lexy paid the fare then got out behind Nans while Ida and Helen scrambled out the other door and Ruth jumped out of the front. It was before eight in the morning, so the place was nearly deserted, except for a rusted-out old orange Jeep parked a short way down.

Ruth smoothed her hand down the front of her old-lady pull-on stretchy jeans then walked over to her storage unit, key in hand, only to stop short. "Well, that's odd."

"What's wrong?" Lexy asked, coming up beside her.

"The padlock on the door." Ruth pointed. "It's not on there."

"Could the owner of the storage facility have removed it for you?" Nans asked, now standing on Ruth's other side. She was a few inches shorter than Lexy and Ruth both, at five feet one.

"Maybe," Ruth said, frowning. "I *did* tell Stan I was coming over this morning to get my Olds."

"Too bad he didn't stick around to help you open the door too," Helen said, staring dubiously at the storage bay, her demeanor regal despite their location. "That thing looks like it weighs a ton."

"Nonsense." Ruth stepped forward and grabbed the handle. "There's nothing to it. Besides, I've been working out, pumping iron in the gym at the retirement home."

"And flirting with that man who wears the nice hats," Ida added with a raised brow. "What's his name again? Harold? Hugo?"

"Herman. Herman Conti." Ruth grabbed the handle on the door and lifted it with one hand, shooting Ida an annoyed stare, as if to prove her point. "See? Easy as pie."

Inside the storage bay sat a 1970s blue Oldsmobile

parked head in, the paint and chrome still sparkling like brand new. The thing was a huge four-door sedan and took up most of the space in the unit. It was so large, in fact, that the ladies all had to sidle in carefully just to reach the doors. Nans and Lexy took the left side while Helen and Ida took the right. Ruth had already run up to the front of the car and stood inspecting the exterior like a seasoned pro.

"Oh, shoot," Ruth said, bent over the front bumper.

"What's wrong?" Nans asked, stopping halfway down the side of the enormous vehicle.

"I've snagged my bracelet on the front fender." Ruth tugged several times then scowled as a metallic tinkling echoed through the storage bay. "Darn it. The clasp broke."

She bent further to retrieve it from the ground then froze. "Oh dear."

Lexy did not like the tone in her voice.

Slowly, she and Nans and the other ladies inched their way toward the front of the vehicle.

"Is your bracelet broken?" Ida asked.

"No. It's not that. It's..." Ruth pointed beneath the vehicle. "There's..."

"What? An oil leak, perhaps?" Nans pulled out her cell phone. "I can give Jeffries Auto Body a call and have them send someone."

"I don't think a mechanic's going to help," Ruth said, the color draining from her cheeks.

"A flat tire then?" Helen crossed her arms.

"No."

"Transmission fluid?" Lexy suggested, her nerves completely on edge now. She needed to get these cream puffs delivered pronto, but given poor Ruth's slightly dazed expression, whatever was happening under the car was quite awful. Maybe the radiator had burst. She wondered if she should put in a call to the cabbie—he must not have gone very far yet.

"No."

Nans flapped her arms as she finally rounded the front of the car. "Oh, come on, Ruth. What is..."

Nans stopped short, and Lexy almost ran into her. Lexy followed Nans' gaze to the floor just under the grill of the car where a pair of black wing-tip shoes were sticking out.

Nans squatted down and peered under the car. "Ruth's right. It's too late to call a mechanic. This guy is dead."

# CHAPTER TWO

*S*tan's Storage wasn't exactly the sort of place where people lingered. Row after row of squatty concrete buildings with large rusted metal doors, separated by the occasional alleyway or chain-link fence. No trees, no shrubs, not even a blade of grass poking up between the rare cracks in the pavement. It was set near a swamp, and a musty smell hung in the air. Insects made buzzing and chirping noises in the overgrown grass. Even the sun seemed not to want to linger, and it dipped behind a cloud, leaving a dim pallor over the area.

With little other choice, Lexy and the ladies sat on a low retaining wall near the curb at the end of the parking area in front of Ruth's storage unit to wait for the authorities. Thankfully, a breeze had picked up, chasing away a swarm of tiny black bugs, two of which had already bitten Lexy. She fiddled with the box on her lap, disappointed she'd now miss her delivery time to the Ladies Auxiliary luncheon. She'd always prided herself on The Cup and Cake's sterling reputation for quality and reliability too.

Her assistant, Cassie, was always getting on Lexy about being too hard on herself, and maybe this was another case of her making herself feel bad about circumstances beyond her control. After all, it wasn't as though she'd gotten out of bed that morning with the goal of finding a dead guy wedged beneath a car.

She sighed and checked her watch. It was nearly eleven now, and the police still hadn't arrived. Their cab driver wasn't answering the phone, which was probably for the best, anyway. She couldn't very well leave the scene, and given the guy's obvious discomfort after more "colorful" aspects of their past had come to light during the drive over, the poor man probably would've passed out if he'd seen the corpse beneath Ruth's Olds.

"Sorry you missed your delivery," Ida said, lifting the corner of the box's lid and trying to look inside. "I hope it isn't anything that would go bad. Because, if so, we might want to make sure they don't go to waste."

Lexy sighed and passed the box over to her. "You might as well eat them before the filling goes bad. They were for delivery to an important client, but it doesn't look like I'll make it there on time now."

"Well," Nans said, patting Lexy on the hand. "I'm sure they'll understand, under the circumstances. Solving crimes should take precedence over anything else, right?"

Wincing, Lexy looked away. Before, she'd always agreed with Nans. Now, given Jack's concerns about her and the ladies' activities, she wasn't so sure anymore.

The ladies each pulled napkins out of their purses. And not flimsy paper ones, either. Each of them seemed to be armed with high-quality linen napkins. Helen's even had embroidery on the edges. They spread them on their laps before daintily taking a cream puff and biting into the flaky pastry as though they were at high tea and not stuck sitting in a stiflingly hot asphalt parking lot that smelled like dry grass and swamp. They each took a puff and passed the box back to Lexy. She was far too tense to eat. She passed the box back to Ida.

"Oh, these are divine, my dear," Nans mumbled around a bite of puff.

"Yes," Helen agreed, dabbing a bit of vanilla cream from the corner of her mouth. "I've always said you have a real talent for the culinary arts."

"Thank you." Lexy smiled, holding her hand over her eyes to shield them from the sun while doing her best to take comfort in the fact the efforts of her labor wouldn't go to waste at least. Sure, the Ladies Auxiliary was an

13

important civic group in Brook Ridge Falls, but she'd make it up to them at some point. Maybe cater the desserts for their next luncheon for free. Yes, it would bite into her bottom line, but if it saved her reputation, then it would be worth it. Decided, she changed subjects. "So does anyone have an idea of the identity of that unfortunate man under Ruth's car?"

"No clue," Ruth said after swallowing her last bite of pastry. "I'd guess from his location, though, that he was trying to inspect the engine. Perhaps he's a mechanic."

"Maybe he wanted to give you a tune-up," Ida said, chuckling. "I know a line of guys at the retirement center who'd gladly volunteer for the task."

"Now is not the time for jokes." Nans gave her friend a scolding look. "There's a dead body in that storage unit, and the police are going to want to know how he got there. We need to figure out what we're going to tell the cops."

As if on cue, sirens wailed, coming closer, and two squad cars pulled into the lot, followed by the crime scene tech van. Soon, officers swarmed the area, including Jack, who gave Lexy a funny look. Her heart sank a bit when he didn't come right over, but he had a job to do, and she wasn't in danger. Besides, judging by the way his brows were drawn down over his brown eyes when he glanced her way, she suspected he wasn't going to have anything comforting to say to her.

They cordoned off Ruth's storage bay and meticulously photographed the scene before starting to remove and bag items for evidence. The ladies discarded their trash then wandered closer to see what was happening. No one had approached them yet for their statements. Lexy exhaled with relief. That would give her time to compose herself. Lately, she'd gotten the distinct impression Jack was not thrilled by her frequent investigations with the Ladies Detective Club.

"Is that a drill?" Ida asked, pointing toward a bag carried by one of the crime scene technicians. "If it is, then he must've been doing something to your car, Ruth."

"From the blood covering the drill bit, I believe that's the murder weapon," Nans said, her gaze narrowed on the power tool. "I'm no expert, though."

Lexy gave her grandmother a look. Nans might not be a sworn law enforcement officer, but she had the instincts of Sherlock Holmes. If she thought that drill was the murder weapon, then chances were good it probably was. To confirm, Lexy leaned closer as the tech walked by them toward the van. She gasped at the bright crimson streaks marring the shiny, slim drill bit. "You're right."

"Of course I am," Nans said, winking. "Now if we

could just get your stubborn husband to admit the same, we'd be all set."

Before Lexy could respond, Jack turned his attention in her direction, and Lexy's heart plummeted to her toes. Jack walked over to their little group, giving his wife a disapproving stare as he approached. Yep. He wasn't happy with her at all. After nodding briefly to the ladies, he pulled Lexy aside.

"I know your car's in the shop, but you should've asked me for a ride earlier. Or asked Cassie. Or even gotten a rental instead of accepting a ride with Mona and her friends. Trouble always seems to follow whenever all of you get together." He gave her a reproachful look. "Why didn't you say anything, honey?"

"Don't be silly. You're always so busy these days. I didn't want to bother you." Lexy laughed, trying to play off his concern, though she sensed his true impatience. "And I did say something. I mentioned last night at dinner that I had to deliver cream puffs to the auxiliary this morning, and it seemed wasteful to rent a car just for one silly errand."

"Where are your cream puffs now?" he asked, crossing his arms and casting a quick glance at the nearby trash can, where the top of the white bakery box with The Cup and Cake's logo poked out. "I can run you wherever you need to go once I'm done here."

Guilty warmth prickled Lexy's cheeks, and it had nothing to do with the sunshine. She stared down at the toes of her cute white flats. "After what happened in the storage facility then the wait for law enforcement to show up, I figured getting the delivery there on time was a long shot at best. The ladies were hungry, so I let them eat the cream puffs rather than having them go to waste."

"I see." Jack's gaze flicked to Ida, who stood watching their conversation with interest as she brushed a few stray pastry flakes from the front of her flowered top. She gave Lexy a wink, her bright-blue eyes sparkling with mischief, as usual. Jack gave a long-suffering sigh and pinched the bridge of his nose between his thumb and forefinger. "Listen, please stay here while I check out the scene, and try not to get into any more trouble, please. After I'm done, I'll give you a ride back to the bakery." He glanced over at Nans with the patience of a saint. His smile was polite, but Lexy didn't miss the spark of irritation in his eyes. "Would you ladies like me to arrange a ride for you back to the retirement home?"

"Don't be ridiculous." Nans scoffed then pulled out her cell phone to wave in his face. "I've already requested an Uber. Should be here shortly. Besides, we've spent enough time gracing the back of your police car, don't you think?"

CHAPTER THREE

*a*n hour and a half later, Jack finally dropped Lexy off in front of The Cup and Cake. She hurried to get out of the car, eager to get back to work. She loved her husband with all her heart, but if he lectured her for one more minute about being at that crime scene, she just might lose it. A heated argument was the last thing she needed to kick off her afternoon.

"Honey, wait." Jack caught her wrist as she opened the door. "You know I'm only saying these things because I love you and I don't want you to get hurt, right?"

Lexy sighed and glanced back at him over her shoulder. "I know, Jack. But I'm a big girl and can take care of myself. And it's not like I go in search of these things. They find me. What am I supposed to do, huh? Just leave the dead body there and walk away?"

"No. I know." Jack exhaled and lowered his head, his

expression pensive. Besides, they both knew asking the ladies to give up their snooping ways was like asking a fish not to swim, and there was no way Lexy was going to let her grandmother traipse all around the countryside to these crime scenes without protection. "At least promise me you and Mona will give law enforcement time to figure out the identity of the victim before you go off on some amateur sleuthing adventure, okay?"

"I'll do my best. That's all I can promise." She gave him a quick peck on the lips then climbed out of the sedan. "I'll see you later at home."

"Yep." He winked as she shut the door then waited until she was inside the bakery before pulling away. Other than his mollycoddling ways where she was concerned, Jack was a sweet, kind, wonderful man, and she thanked her lucky stars every day for their marriage.

Back in her element, Lexy smiled as she walked inside her shop, inhaling the warm smell of freshly baked cookies. Her spirits rose as she looked at the glass bakery case loaded with brownies, cookies, scones, and cakes all arranged on doilies and sitting on pedestals or lined up on trays.

She glanced back outside through the large front windows to see the waterfall across the street. That view was one of the reasons she'd fallen in love with the building. Right now, some of her patrons were sitting at the wrought-iron cafe tables she'd set up on the sidewalk in front of the window, sipping coffee, eating pastries, and enjoying that same view.

Cassie, her best friend, was ringing someone up. The cash register dinged as she closed the drawer, and the customer walked away happily with the white bag clutched to their chest. Lexy and Cassie had been inseparable since ninth grade, and now Cassie's husband, John, was Jack's partner in the police department. Her help had been indispensable to Lexy in the daily operation of the bakery... and even on a few investigations.

"Hey," she said as Lexy approached, the midafternoon sun glinting off the neon turquoise of her hair. It was a change from her usual pink hues but suited Cassie perfectly. Cassie was adventurous and quirky when it came to clothing and hairstyles. The opposite of Lexy, who never strayed far from her mink-brown color or the sleek, standard ponytail she always wore her long hair in or the earth-toned tee shirts and plain denim jeans she favored. "How'd it go with the Ladies Auxiliary?"

"Unfortunately, I never made it. We ran into a... *situation* on the way there." Lexy stowed her purse under the counter then walked over to the hooks on the wall to choose her apron for the day. She'd been collecting vintage aprons since she'd started the shop and now had quite an impressive collection. For today, she picked an adorable one that was covered in bright-red cherries and had a ruffle and a large pocket on the front. She forced a smile as she joined Cassie behind the counter again.

"What kind of a situation? I could have delivered them," Cassie said, frowning. In a small town like Brook Ridge Falls, not everyone was as tolerant as Lexy, so there was a reason she usually made the deliveries to the local Ladies Auxiliary. She doubted the conservative group would appreciate her friend's colorful displays of her inner creativity. Not that she'd ever tell her friend that. "Not another crime, I hope."

When Lexy didn't say anything, Cassie pounced. "Another one? Seriously, Lexy. I'm beginning to think you're a magnet for these things or something."

The words hit a bit too close to home for Lexy, considering what she'd just been through with Jack. Not wanting to rehash it all again, she turned to wipe down the already pristine counters.

"What about the cream puffs? I don't see the box."

Lexy gave her friend a look and continued wiping.

"Fine." Cassie crossed her arms and leaned her hip against the wall. "Out with it. Whatever this *situation* you encountered this morning was, it must've been stressful considering you downed a dozen of your own desserts."

"I didn't eat them," Lexy said. She'd long ago learned

not to sample her merchandise if she wanted any hope of retaining her figure. "It was Nans and her friends who ate them all. In fact, they each had at least two. I'm sure Ida had three, and I think I saw Helen stuff one or two in her purse for later."

"I still don't understand why you didn't have me run you over to the auxiliary."

"Because I needed you here to handle the morning rush. You know that." Lexy threw her hands up in exasperation. "Sorry if I sound short. I just got a lecture from Jack."

Cassie waited a few seconds then asked, "So what happened?"

"There was a dead body in Ruth's storage unit. *That's* what happened."

"What?" Cassie's voice echoed through the quiet— and now thankfully empty—shop. "A dead body? Who was it? How did it get there? Is Jack investigating?"

Lexy bit back a smile at her friend's barrage of questions. She was every bit as inquisitive as Lexy was, if a bit less discreet about it. There was a reason they'd become best friends.

She tossed the washrag back under the counter then faced Cassie. "Ruth opened the door to the storage bay where she keeps her Oldsmobile and discovered a man under her car. Dead. Only his wing-tip shoes sticking out from beneath the front fender. No idea how he got there, though the lock wasn't on the overhead door when we arrived. No identity for the victim yet. Naturally, the cops are investigating."

"How awful!" Cassie shuddered.

"Yeah. Not exactly the way I like to start my days." Lexy turned as the bells above the front door jangled merrily. Nans and the ladies walked in. A large silver and wood-grained station wagon sat near the curb, the driver locking the doors with her key fob.

Cassie grinned. "Speak of the devil."

"Lexy, so glad you made it here," Nans said, winking. "I hope Jack wasn't too hard on you."

"He wasn't too bad." Lexy watched Ida push her way through the group to stand in front of the display case. For such a petite lady, she had the appetite of a giant. Ruth and Helen soon joined her to peruse the daily selection of goodies. The bells jangled again as the driver entered. A woman with dyed-red hair and an ample bosom. Lexy didn't recognize her. Must be one of the many retirement home residents, she figured. And apparently an Uber driver.

Helen gestured to the redhead. "Lexy, have you met our new friend Myra Stoddard?"

"No, I don't believe I have." She shook the woman's

hand. "Very nice to meet you, Myra. Do you live at the retirement community as well?"

"Excuse me?" Myra cupped her ear, her charm bracelet tinkling as she tilted her head toward Lexy.

"You'll have to speak up," Ida said. "Myra doesn't hear so good. Had to keep repeating the directions to her in the car."

Lexy repeated the question a little louder.

"Yes. My husband, Joe, and I just moved into one of the lovely condos." She pointed out the windows to the station wagon. "I'm not quite ready to retire yet, so I do some Uber driving on the side to supplement our income. We need all the money we can get right now since my husband's recent hernia surgery. Got to pay off those bills."

"Joe makes the loveliest jewelry." Ruth leaned closer to Lexy to show off her copper earrings. "He made me these beauties from several old coins I had lying around that I thought were pretty. He made my bracelet too, the one I broke back in the storage unit."

At the mention of the crime scene, a pall seemed to fall over the group.

"So what's the special today?" Ida asked at last, peering in at all the baked goods.

"The double-fudge brownies," Cassie said. "We have them with and without walnuts."

"I'll take one with nuts, please." Ida pulled out her wallet. "That one in the last row with all the crispy edges."

"That sounds good to me too," Nans said. "I'd like a smaller one, though, please."

"Me three." Myra stepped forward. "And put all their orders on my bill."

The ladies protested, but Myra was having none of it.

"That's very nice of you," Lexy said, ringing up their purchases while Cassie got their orders ready. She glanced up, noticing the woman's trendy clothes and expensive handbag. Uber driving must pay pretty well if that gigantic silver-dollar necklace and matching earrings were any indication. "I'm sure the ladies appreciate it."

"Of course. Anything for my friends." Myra smiled, handing Lexy the money. "Keep the change. Oh, that reminds me, Ruth. Joe gave me these for you too." She pulled a small blue box from her purse. "The new earrings you had made."

"Oh, thank you!" Ruth opened the box and held it out for all of them to see. Inside were a set of buffalo nickels on sterling posts, with the background cut out so only the buffalos and the rim of the coins remained. "Aren't they pretty?"

"Lovely." Lexy pointed toward the far wall. "And, ladies, help yourselves to the coffee and tea. My treat."

Ida, Helen, and Ruth headed over to get their drinks while Nans lingered near the counter. "Can you take a short break and join us, dear?" she asked Lexy. "We need to discuss what happened... *earlier*."

"Oh, I don't know." Lexy glanced over at Cassie, feeling guilty. "I just got back in, and there's so much still left to do in the back and—"

"Go ahead," Cassie said, waving her off. "I'm fine."

"Are you sure?"

"Yep. I've got another batch of brownies due out of the oven in about five minutes anyway, so take all the time you need."

"Okay." Lexy walked outside with her grandmother and took a seat at the umbrella-covered table near the end of the patio with the other women. From her seat, she'd be able to see if anyone came into the bakery and could jump up to help them while Cassie was in the kitchen. The day was flooded with spring sunshine that warmed up the street. The slight breeze brought the smell of lilacs, and a pair of sparrows hopped around on the sidewalk, their shiny black eyes darting hopefully at the ladies' pastries as they waited for crumbs to drop.

"Such a shame about finding that body this morning,"

Helen said after swallowing a bite of her brownie. "I do hope the police find out who he is soon."

"Yes, me too. That way I can get my car back," Ruth said. "I miss driving."

"Why?" Ida asked, sipping her tea. "Got a hot date?"

"Don't be ridiculous," Ruth scoffed. "You know I haven't dated anyone seriously since Nunzio."

"That's it!" Nans said, snapping her fingers. "I've been trying to think of why that man would've been in Ruth's storage unit, poking around her car. I bet Nunzio is the connection. He was murdered for blackmailing those other crime bosses, right?"

Ruth straightened her blouse, her cheeks a slight pink. "Yes, but he wasn't a bad man. I mean, maybe he was sort of bad, but he was good to me."

Ida's left brow flew up. "And that list was never found, was it?"

"No," Ruth shook her head.

"Could be that man in the storage unit was looking for the list because he was on it and didn't want his sins of the past to come back to haunt him," Nans said.

Ruth frowned. "Don't be silly, Mona. Why in the world would anyone think Nunzio's list was in the car? The cops searched far and wide for it after Nunzio died and never found it. What makes you think some strange man could waltz in and locate it just like that?"

"She's got a point," Helen said.

"Didn't you say Nunzio always told you to make sure you took good care of that car?" Nans asked, one brow raised. "Perhaps his concern was for more than your well-being."

"Well, yes, he said that, but that was only because it was in such good condition. He said it was a cream puff and—" Ruth sputtered.

"Hiding the list in the Olds?" Ida interrupted. "Oh, that's brilliant!"

"Now, wait a minute," Lexy said, doing her best to rein the ladies in so she could keep her promise to Jack. "The police haven't even identified the victim. We should let them do their jobs first before we come up with all these wild theories."

"Of course, dear." Nans nudged her with her shoulder. "This is all just conjecture at this point. But think about it. Why else would anyone want to break into Ruth's vehicle storage unit? Maybe what we should focus on at this point isn't the murder, but whether or not the killer found what they were looking for."

# CHAPTER FOUR

T he ladies stayed for about an hour before calling for another Uber ride to go home. This time, someone other than Myra showed up. They seemed to be enjoying this mode of transportation. Maybe, after this, Ruth would give up driving. She might have to if the police kept her car. Maybe Lexy should try Uber. She had no idea how long her car would be in the shop or if it was even fixable.

It was nearly closing time when Lexy's phone buzzed in her apron pocket. She'd been cleaning out the display cases to get things ready for the next day. They packaged up the day-old pastries and gave them to the homeless shelter. Well, those that Nans and the ladies didn't swing by to claim. But Nans hadn't come back, and Jack was due to be there any minute to pick her up.

She pulled the phone out and glanced at the screen then frowned. Scratch that. Jack was cancelling on her. His text said he had to work late.

Disappointed, she removed her apron then locked the front door and headed into the back of the store, thankful Cassie was still there. At least she could always count on her best friend. Which was good considering how Jack had been making a habit of cancelling on her lately. "Hey, can I catch a ride home with you?"

"Uh, sure." Cassie finished shutting down the ovens. "What happened to Jack?"

"He just sent me a message. Has to work late tonight."

"Oh." Cassie turned away to search for something under the sink. "No problem."

Maybe it was for the best, Lexy reasoned as she grabbed her purse from the front and took off her apron. Given the tension between them before, a little time apart could be just what they needed. Never mind the tugging ache in her heart over missing Jack. She'd see him again soon enough. Lexy did one more walk-through to make sure everything was secure, then they went out the back exit to the alley, where Cassie was parked.

"How's John doing?" Lexy asked as she climbed into the passenger seat of Cassie's Prius. "Is he working late too?"

"Not that I know of. Why?"

"Just wondered. Since they've got that new case and all. Seems like if Jack was working late, John would be too."

"Hmm." Cassie started the engine then pulled out of the alley. "John didn't really say anything about it when I talked to him earlier. He might have forgotten to mention it. Or maybe he's doing cleanup on an older case."

Cassie changed the subject to the new fondant colors they'd started experimenting with, pink-and-purple swirls and rainbow. They'd been working on ways to wrap the fondant over a cake and not have any creases in the pattern. Twenty minutes later, Cassie dropped Lexy off in front of her craftsman-style bungalow. She'd left a light on in the front living room, and she spotted her dog, Sprinkles, in the front window, tail wagging in anticipation.

After a quick goodbye and thank you to Cassie, she let herself inside. Sprinkles met her at the door—all wagging tail and floppy white fur. She scampered around in circles, her nails clicking on the hardwood floor, until Lexy picked her up to cuddle. Through the cozy living room, she spotted her prized grandfather clock against the dining room wall. It was a bit after six. "How's my baby tonight, huh?"

Sprinkles nuzzled her soft fur against Lexy's neck and then covered her chin in sloppy dog kisses.

"Yech." Lexy put Sprinkles down gently and wiped her chin.

She headed into the kitchen with Sprinkles leaping around her feet. She refilled the dog's food and water bowls before letting Sprinkles out into the fenced backyard for some exercise. The black-and-white linoleum gleamed merrily, and the crisp white cabinets beckoned. She'd just started pulling things out of the fridge for dinner when Jack walked through the front door, wine and flowers in hand.

"I'm so sorry about not being able give you a ride tonight, honey." He kissed her sweetly, setting his items on the granite countertop so he could slide his arms around her waist. All Lexy's anxiety about Jack's cancellation melted away. There was no better place in the world than where Lexy was right that minute. She rested her palm against his chest to feel the steady thump of his heartbeat. Jack smiled down at her. "How was your day?"

"Good. You'll be happy to know there was no more snooping at all," she teased. "Your stern warning worked."

He winced. "I'm sorry about that too. I didn't mean to be so hard on you. I just worry about you when I'm not around."

"I know." She kissed him again then pulled away to

let Sprinkles back inside. "And I appreciate that. And the gifts." She gestured toward the beautiful pink roses—her favorite—and the wine. "Is this to apologize for earlier, or were you being naughty too?"

"What? No." He shook his head and turned away fast, his expression flustered. "I just like doing nice things for you, honey. What are we making for dinner?"

"How about baked chicken and potatoes?"

"Sounds great." He joined her at the counter, and they prepared the food together. Jack scrubbed the potatoes then doused them in olive oil and salt and pepper before poking them with a fork and wrapping them in foil. Lexy cleaned the chicken breasts then doused them in olive oil and garlic before she dredged them in bread crumbs and Parmesan cheese. They went into a stoneware baker then into the oven with the potatoes to bake for an hour.

Jack uncorked the wine and poured them each a glass, handing one to Lexy after she finished washing and drying her hands. "We discovered the identity of the victim from this morning."

"Yeah?" she said, sipping her chardonnay and trying to act nonchalant. "Who was he?"

"Guy by the name of Sherman Wilson," Jack said.

"Like the paint?" Lexy asked.

"No. That's Sherwin Williams, honey." Jack laughed.

"We had a few chuckles around the station about that too, until we got his background check. Turns out the guy robbed a bank. Just got out of jail for it too." Jack took a swallow of his wine then frowned. "Which doesn't explain why a man who's fresh out of prison would be found dead under Ruth's car. Can't imagine a guy who just finished serving his time in prison would go right back to being involved in a robbery that could send him back behind bars."

"Huh. That does seem odd, doesn't it? Unless he was desperate." Lexy took Jack's hand and led him into the living room, where they both took a seat on the over-stuffed sofa. "The ladies stopped by again for brownies at the bakery this afternoon."

"Yeah?" Jack set his glass on the coffee table, one side of his full lips quirking into a smile. "And here I thought you said you weren't snooping again."

"I wasn't. Honest." She gave him a gentle, reproachful look. "Nans did bring up a good point, though, while they were eating."

"What's that?"

"She mentioned Nunzio and his blackmail list. You guys never did find it, did you?"

"Nope." Jack narrowed his gaze. "Why?"

"Well, her theory was what if this Wilson man knew about the list and came looking for it once he was freed from prison? After all, criminals do talk on the inside, right? Nans thought maybe this Sherman Wilson was on the list, or maybe he wanted to find it so he could continue Nunzio's blackmail scheme."

Jack shook his head and exhaled slowly, his expression resigned. "Figures Mona and the ladies would be right in the thick of things again. Listen, honey. I want you to promise me you'll stay out of this one, all right? This Wilson guy was a dangerous criminal—clever, resourceful, ruthless. Which means whoever killed him must have been even worse to get the upper hand on him. I don't want you or Mona or any of her friends from the retirement community to get any crazy ideas about helping on this investigation. The Brook Ridge Falls Police Department is perfectly capable of handling this investigation on our own. After all, I'm the homicide detective in the family, remember?"

He pulled her into his arms and kissed her before getting up to grab the wine from the kitchen. When he returned, he poured them each a refill before continuing. "Hey, since your car's still in the shop and I couldn't pick you up after work tonight, how about I get up early in the morning and drop you at the bakery?" He clinked wine glasses with her. "Sound good?"

"Yes." Lexy smiled, glad to have their easy connection back again. "I'd like that."

"Good. And I want you to promise me you'll stay at the shop all day tomorrow. The last thing I need is for you to go out snooping with your grandmother and risking life and limb, not until we get whoever's responsible for Sherman Wilson's murder behind bars. Okay?"

Lexy ducked her head, a twinge of remorse pinching her chest. She loved Jack more than life itself, but him asking her to promise something like that was impossible. Not when she was certain the ladies would be back out in force the next day. She couldn't leave Nans and her friends to their own devious devices, especially after what Jack had said about Wilson's killer.

"Great." Jack toed off his shoes and stretched out his long legs, slipping his arm around Lexy's shoulders and snuggling her into his side. Sprinkles jumped up on the sofa and settled in beside Lexy to sleep. Jack kissed Lexy on the top of the head then clicked on the TV news. "Let's watch some news while we wait for supper to cook."

While the reporter on-screen rattled off the day's top headlines, Lexy's mind raced. Lying to her husband didn't sit well with her. Then again, she hadn't verbally agreed to not see Nans and her friends the next day, so that wouldn't constitute an actual promise, would it? As of now, she had no plans to leave the bakery tomorrow, but that could change on a dime where the Ladies Detective Club was concerned.

She cuddled against Jack's warmth and deeply inhaled his scent—musk and vanilla and trust—before sighing. Nope. No promises. That way she wouldn't have to break her word to him again.

# CHAPTER FIVE

The morning sun slanted in through the front window of The Cup and Cake, glinting off the stainless-steel edging of the pastry display case, the glass of which Lexy had just spent ten minutes getting squeaky clean. Inside, a fresh batch of croissants battled with cheese Danishes and blueberry scones for attention. On the top shelf, three dozen cinnamon rolls so fresh from the oven that the air was still spiced with their scent dripped with glaze.

Lexy stood back to admire the display. *Would the elephant ears look better in the center of the shelf or to the right? Center.* She went to the back of the case, slid the door open, and had her upper body inside the case, trying to reach the platter of rolls, when the bells over the door jingled.

She peered through the front of the case, the curved

glass distorting the image of a dapper older gentleman in a tweed sport coat and a slightly battered fedora coming through the door.

Lexy extracted herself from the case and smiled a greeting.

He raised his cane to her in greeting. "Good morning, my dear. Lovely day we're having. Just lovely."

"Hello," Lexy said, wiping her hands on her vintage pink polka-dot apron. "How may I help you today?"

"Oh, well, I've never been to the bakery and thought I'd pop in to see what you had to offer. I've heard such good things about your baked goods." He removed his hat, revealing a bald patch amidst his curly gray hair. "And I must say it smells wonderful in here."

"Thank you." Lexy couldn't help smiling at the old charmer. He was right. Cassie had some almond scones going in the oven, and the air was heavy with the scent of sugar and almonds mingled with the cinnamon from the rolls. "Are you living at the retirement center?"

Given the small size of Brook Ridge Falls, the geriatrics made up a sizable portion of her customer base, and most of them lived at the senior center, but Lexy had met a good portion of the residents. Then again, the woman who had driven the Uber car was new to her, so this gentleman could be too.

"No, my dear, I have my own place. How lovely this

bakery is—you must be a hard worker." He gave her a coy look. "You must keep your husband on his toes."

"I try." Lexy winked and held out her hand. "I'm Lexy Baker."

"Herman Conti," the man said, taking her hand and bowing. "At your service."

"Very nice to meet you, Mr. Conti." She walked behind the counter. "My grandmother is part of the retirement community. She lives at the center. Perhaps you know her. Mona—"

"My dear, who do you think talked up your establishment to me?" Herman smiled. "She and her friends are quite a riot."

"Hmm." The conversation from the taxi the previous day ran through Lexy's head. If she wasn't mistaken, Mr. Conti was the gentleman Ida had teased Ruth about, saying he was sweet on her. Considering her last boyfriend was a gangster, it looked as if Ruth could do a lot worse than Mr. Conti.

"What can I get for you today? My assistant is in the back, getting a fresh batch of almond scones ready, if you'd like. Or perhaps a box of freshly baked cookies to take back home?"

"Hmm." He perused the selections in the case then straightened. "For now, I believe I'll wait on some of those scones, if you don't mind."

Lexy gestured to one of the empty tables near the window. "Have a seat. They should be out shortly."

"Thank you." Mr. Conti took off his hat and laid it on the chair next to him. "You know, your grandmother and her friends are the reason I'm here today."

"Really?" Lexy said, going back to her rearranging. "Besides the food recommendation."

"Yes. You see, I'm good friends with one of your grandmother's dear friends. Ruth. I came here this morning hoping I might see her. Has she been in yet today?"

"I'm afraid not, Mr. Conti." Lexy smiled at his earnest tone. Seemed the old guy had it bad for Ruth. "But I can let her know you came by if I see her later."

"Oh, no need. No need. I was just worried about her after all that fuss at her storage unit yesterday."

Lexy straightened, frowning. "You heard about that?"

"News travels fast in a small town," he said, toying with the end of his cane. "Good and bad. Anyway, I just wanted to make sure she was all right."

"Well, if it's any consolation, as far as I know, she's fine. I was there with them yesterday when the body was discovered, and though it was quite shocking, I think we'll all survive."

"Excellent to hear, my dear."

Mr. Conti didn't look quite as enthused as his statement suggested, and she felt a pang of pity for him. "I'll certainly let Ruth know of your concern for her, though, if I see her."

"Oh, thank you." He perked up a bit, looking around the bakery. "I used to own my own business once. A men's hat shop. This was when the Rat Pack had hit it big. Sold a lot of fedoras back then. Even headed my local Rotary Club chapter. Good times then."

His expression turned melancholy, and Lexy wanted to ask him more but never got the chance.

"Fresh, hot scones coming up," Cassie said, carrying out a tray filled with almond, ham, and blueberry scones. She glanced over and saw their guest. "Oh hi, Mr. Conti. Don't you look handsome today."

He puffed up like a peacock. "Flattery, dear, will get you everywhere. And isn't that shade of blue on your tresses just perfect with your complexion."

Cassie gave him a curtsy then grinned at Lexy. "Have I mentioned how much I love working here?"

"Not recently, no." Lexy took the tray and fit it into an empty space in the display case. Afterward, she turned back to Mr. Conti. "Scones are ready. How many would you like, sir?"

"An even half dozen, please. I'll take a few to the senior center to share with the other residents." Mr. Conti stood and pulled out his wallet to pay. "And give me a dozen of those snickerdoodle cookies too. Always love a good snickerdoodle."

Lexy rang up his purchases and handed him his change then leaned her forearms on the counter as she watched him put the money back in his pocket. His clothes had to be at least thirty years old, given their wear, but his watch looked new and shiny. Odd. But then maybe he'd gotten it as a gift recently.

"Don't forget to tell Ruth I asked about her," he said, picking up his box of goodies. "From what I saw on the news this morning, the police are still searching for the killer. Dangerous stuff, that."

"Will do, Mr. Conti. And you be careful out there yourself." She smiled and waved as he headed for the door. "Have a good day, and it was wonderful to meet you."

He left, and Lexy turned back to Cassie, who was leaning against the back wall behind the counter with her arms crossed. "So you love working here, huh?"

"Sometimes," Cassie joked back. "When my boss isn't grilling me."

"Nice." Lexy walked back into the kitchen with Cassie on her heels.

"Good thing I gave you a ride home yesterday," Cassie said, adjusting the temperature on the oven for the next batch of goodies going in—giant cupcakes they would use to make Lexy's famous cupcake tops. "The boys worked late last night, huh?"

"Late?" Lexy gave her friend a confused stare. "Jack came home right after you dropped me off."

"Really?" Cassie seemed flustered. "Oh, well. I guess I thought he'd be late because John didn't get in until after nine. He wouldn't tell me about his day either. Did Jack act strangely last night?"

"No. Not really. Why?"

"Nothing." Cassie gave the dark chocolate batter in a stainless steel bowl a few swipes with a spatula. She poured it carefully into the paper-lined muffin pan then slid it into the oven. "Never mind."

The whole exchange was weird and left Lexy feeling more than a little unsettled. Images of Jack arriving with roses and wine flashed in her head. Come to think of it, he'd never brought her gifts before when he'd been late. Nor had he apologized when they'd had a minor disagreement. And when she'd asked him if he'd been naughty, he'd gotten all flustered...

The phone on the wall rang, jarring her out of her thoughts. Lexy answered, scolding herself for being silly. Jack was wonderful and sweet and kind and caring. There was nothing suspicious going on. She was creating mountains out of mole hills... "The Cup and Cake. Lexy speaking. How may I—"

"Lexy, dear. It's Nans."

Her voice sounded frantic, and Lexy's pulse skyrocketed. Why hadn't Nans called her cell? "What's wrong?"

"There's trouble at Ruth's condo at the retirement community. Can you come over?"

"I'll be right there." She hung up and ripped off her apron. "I need to get to Nans' right away. Can I borrow your car?"

"Uh, sure." Cassie followed her out to the front of the shop, where Lexy grabbed her purse from beneath the counter. "Is everything all right?"

"I'm not sure," Lexy said, grabbing Cassie's keys and heading toward the back exit. "I'll let you know once I find out more."

# CHAPTER SIX

*L*exy's heart was racing like a thoroughbred making its debut run in the Preakness as she careened into the retirement center parking lot. Where were the police cars? The ambulance? She'd expected people to be swarming. The state police. Reporters. Maybe even a medicopter. But there was only one police car, and it didn't even have the lights on. Her anxiety eased down a few notches. Things weren't as bad as she'd imagined.

She'd barely made it into the entrance of the building when she ran into Jack. He did not look happy. Had something happened to Nans? But she'd sounded fine on the phone. Ruth, maybe? Her mind racing and her heart in her throat, she didn't resist as he led her to a quiet corner in the lobby.

"Is Ruth okay?" she asked once they were alone.

"Nans called in a panic, and I got here as fast as I could, but I had to borrow Cassie's car and—"

"She's fine, honey." Jack rubbed her arms until she calmed down a bit. "We're just finishing up. From the looks of things now, it's a simple case of breaking and entering."

"Breaking and entering?" Once her pulse slowed and her breath grew more even, Lexy hazarded a look into her husband's eyes. She'd promised to stay at the bakery all day, and now here she was, blatantly violating their agreement. "I had to come. When Nans called me, so upset, I had to make sure everything was all right. Are you mad I'm here?"

"No," Jack said then sighed. "I would've called you if anything truly bad happened. You know that, right?"

"Yes, I know." Lexy dug the toe of her blue-striped Keds into the carpet. "I guess when the call came in, I just went into autopilot, fearing she might be in danger. With a killer loose and all, I didn't want to take any chances."

"I'm all for eliminating risk. Especially where you're concerned." He smiled then grew serious. "But this is all the more reason for you to stay put from now on. This is too much of a coincidence considering what happened with Ruth's car. The killer could be getting careless. It's too dangerous for you to be showing up at every crime scene in Brook Ridge Falls."

She nodded, and they shared a quick kiss before Nans rushed over. "Jack, do you think what happened today at Ruth's condo had anything to do with the homicide at the storage unit?" Nans asked, her tone low as she eyed the nearby residents.

"I can't discuss an active case, Mona." Jack shoved his hands into his pockets and gave Lexy's grandmother his best stern-cop look. "You know that."

"Is there a lot of damage to Ruth's place?" Lexy looked from Jack to Nans.

"I need to get back to the station," Jack said, backing away from them and avoiding her question. "I'm sure your grandmother can fill you in. See you later, honey. And remember our agreement."

She waved to her husband and then turned back to Nans. "So what happened?"

"Someone tossed Ruth's condo. *That's* what happened," Nans said, scowling. "Ruth's angry, and I don't blame her. This makes the second time someone's done that to her, and she's sick of it."

Lexy bit back the fact that perhaps if Ruth made better choices when it came to her male companions, she might not have to deal with less-than-scrupulous folks. If only she'd fall for that sweet old Mr. Conti. He seemed like a fine, upstanding man.

Ida wandered over and joined in the conversation. "Well, at least the last time, the thieves put away her groceries."

Helen walked up to the group as well, sniffing with disdain. "That's because those burglars were gentlemen. These riff-raff had no manners whatsoever."

Ruth finished giving her statement to one of the officers and came over at last, looking both flustered and furious.

"Are you all right?" Lexy asked her. "Maybe you should sit down for a bit."

"Yes, I'm fine. Thank goodness. And no, I don't want to sit. I want to find the people responsible for this and make them pay."

Hoping to steer the group toward safer water, Lexy changed subjects entirely. "I met a friend of yours this morning, Ruth. Herman Conti. He seemed very nice and worried about you too. He'll be glad to hear you're all right."

"Herman?" Nans, Ida, and Helen said in unison, giving Ruth a suspicious stare.

"Well, you all know he's been coming around my place more lately. As a matter of fact, I also ran into him early this morning, and he wanted to know if I was going to be around for brunch. Of course, I told him I had other plans. I'm not interested in him that way. He's been sweet on me for years, but when I was with Nunzio, he steered clear. Nunzio had warned me to stay away from him too. He was always so very jealous, you know." Ruth blushed, babbling. "Anyway, I'm not going to hook up with Herman or anything. It's just nice to have the attention again, now that Nunzio is gone. Besides, Vincenzio's has a two-for-one early-bird special, so it makes sense to go with someone."

"Hmm." Nans still sounded skeptical but miraculously let the matter drop. Instead, she turned to Lexy. "Spill what you know about the victim from Jack, dear."

Lexy told them what she'd learned about Sherman Wilson and his recent stay in prison. "Jack thinks that it would take another criminal to murder him in cold blood like that."

"Can't say I disagree." Nans began pacing, her gaze narrowed with deep concentration. "Right. Well, I'm going to make an educated guess that there was only one killer in that storage hangar."

"Why's that?" Ida asked.

"It's far too tight in there for more than one person to act with any certainty."

"Makes sense," Helen said. "Also makes sense that if whoever broke into the unit and killed Wilson didn't find what they were looking for, they came here to Ruth's to search for the list. That connects those two dots."

"Again I ask, why in the world would anyone think I had Nunzio's list?" Ruth frowned, clasping her hands in front of her. "If he'd hidden it at my place, I'd have found it during my spring cleaning. I turned the whole apartment upside down. Besides, we spent most of our time at his place, anyway. If the thieves are going to search anywhere, it should be Nunzio's old home."

"But the police searched there with a fine-tooth comb, and besides, someone else lives there now, and it's been renovated," Helen said. "Nothing to be found there."

"What are we going to do next?" Ida asked the rest of the group. "The killer's still out there. What if he comes after Ruth?"

"We won't let that happen," Lexy said, her tone adamant. "The police are working on it, and Jack's putting in overtime to get this case solved. He thinks we should let them handle it and keep ourselves safe."

"Nonsense," Nans said. "If this person is coming after my family and friends, the only way we're going to stay safe is to catch this criminal ourselves. With all their rules and regulations, the police aren't able to act as quickly as we can. And bless Jack's heart, but he'd get a lot further along on his cases if he'd learn to take my advice instead of ignoring it."

"But, Nans—" Lexy started.

"I agree," Helen said. "We've taken matters into our own hands before, and things have always worked out in the end. I'd say we need to start by locating this missing list of Nunzio's." She lowered her voice as several residents of the center walked by, heading to water aerobics. "Maybe it really is hidden in that car somewhere. The guy that ended up dead underneath it probably had some kind of a tip."

"Not to mention the killer," Nans added. "Don't forget, two people were in that storage unit. I don't think that was coincidence. They must have had a reason to be sniffing around Ruth's car."

"Right. Once we have the list, then we can double-check the names and figure out who's still alive and not in prison. One of them must be the killer," Helen said.

"Great plan, except we can't just waltz back into the crime scene, Columbo," Ida said. "The police still have the storage unit cordoned off and guarded, and the Olds is still being searched by the techs."

"True," Helen said. "And I'd much prefer if you called me Miss Marple. Trench-coat beige has never been my color."

Ida rolled her eyes.

"Ladies, I really don't think this is such a good idea," Lexy said, trying to protect the ladies while still keeping her agreement with Jack. "Why don't you all come back with me to the bakery, and we can—"

"Maybe I can call Stan, the storage facility owner, again and see if he can get us in after closing time," Ruth offered, ignoring Lexy completely. "He seemed amenable enough to me when I talked to him last time."

"Perfect." Nans nodded. "And ask him if he saw anyone suspicious sneaking around your unit within the last couple of days. If we can get a description, that might help us narrow down our roster of suspects. C'mon, ladies. While Ruth's doing that, we can use the white board in my condo to lay out what we know so far and plan out our strategy."

Lexy sighed, lingering behind as the ladies took off for the elevators. Part of her wanted to run alongside them and catch another criminal. The other part of her feared that if she broke her promise to Jack again, it might be one step too far. What they had was so precious and sweet and wonderful. Did she really want to risk losing all that?

Then again, Nans had been there for her when no one else had. Nans was her rock. She couldn't just let her and her friends hunt down a killer alone. They'd come after Ruth twice now. What if next time they actually reached her? Lexy shuddered from the horrible thought.

Nans stopped and called back, "Are you coming, dear? We need you."

Lexy hesitated for a second, then, her mind made up, she sprinted to catch up with Nans.

# CHAPTER SEVEN

Once inside Nans' condo, the ladies burst into action. Helen dragged the old stainless steel percolator out from one of the kitchen cabinets and got coffee going. The pot heated quickly, and soon, the smell of dark roast hung in the air, and the pop, pop, pop of the percolator made background noise.

Nans and Ruth pulled an oversized whiteboard on wheels out from the spare room, into the dining room.

Ida rummaged through Nans' fridge, bent at the waist to inspect the contents of the shelves up close. "Hey, Mona, don't you have any leftover pastries?" She shot a look at Lexy over her shoulder as if beaming disapproval that Lexy hadn't thought to bring them a fresh batch when she rushed over.

"In the cheese drawer," Nans said without looking away from the whiteboard, where she was making columns for suspects and clues. The dry-erase marker squeaked along as she drew the lines, and Lexy caught a whiff of stale alcohol from the marker.

"We don't have much to go on," Ida said as she set an etched-glass platter filled with cookies on Nans' mahogany table. She took a seat, a cookie on a dessert plate in front of her, and dug in.

"We know someone was after something in Ruth's car," Nans said.

"And that the victim just got out of jail, so there's a criminal element involved," Helen added.

"And that we need to get to Stan's and see if he has any clues." Ruth pulled her phone out. "I'll call him."

Stan said they could swing by in twenty minutes, and all faces turned toward Lexy. A twinge of guilt pierced her stomach. She'd already spent too much time away from the bakery, and she'd promised Jack she'd mind her own business.

"Sorry, I have to return Cassie's car before she reports it stolen," Lexy said. "Not to mention I have a business to run."

"But what about going to Stan's?" Nans asked, following her out of the dining room and toward the door. "Can't you give us a ride?"

"I'm sorry," Lexy said, bending to kiss her grandmother's cheek. "I can't."

"Oh. Well, wait a minute then." She rushed back into the dining room and returned moments later with her phone in hand. Nans squinted over the tops of her glasses at the screen as she fumbled with typing in a text.

"Who are you messaging?" Lexy asked.

"Our new favorite Uber driver, Myra Stoddard." Nans moved her face closer to the phone. "Darn. I have to start over."

"Let me see that." Ida grabbed the phone. "I'm a wiz at texting. Comes from being a cryptologist in my younger days. I can even do it without looking." As if to prove her point, she closed her eyes, thumbed in the text, then turned the phone around to show them the perfectly worded text. "See."

So much for thinking the ladies could be slowed down. When they had something to investigate, nothing stopped them. Lexy sighed. "I'm really sorry I can't take you ladies to snoop, but I had to borrow Cassie's car to get here, and we're swamped at the bakery, so I really should get back soon, and I promised Jack I wouldn't—"

"Nonsense, dear," Nans said, glancing up at her. "It's no problem whatsoever. I... just... need... to... finish..." She tapped the screen a few more times then smiled. "Done. I sent a message off to Myra about giving us a ride to Stan's place. Now we just have to wait and see when she can pick us up." Her phone buzzed with an incoming response almost immediately. "Well, that didn't take long at all." She turned to call into the dining room, "Myra said she'd be happy to take us, ladies. We just need to walk down to her and Joe's place." Then she turned back to Lexy. "She's always looking to give people rides."

Apparently, with this new Uber thing, the ladies didn't need her anymore. Lexy should have been glad. Nans and her friends often depended on Lexy to drive them, but now they were more independent. But instead of feeling glad, Lexy felt empty. Even though she usually ended up in trouble, she liked being a part of Nans and the ladies' investigations.

Helen unplugged the percolator, the ladies collected their giant patent-leather purses, and they all exited Nans' condo and headed back down to the lobby.

"When did you start texting, Nans?" Lexy asked her grandmother.

"Since I got this new smart phone. I like it so far, but I'm not very good at the messaging part yet. That darned keypad is just so small. Makes it hard to see what I'm typing."

Lexy walked with them out of the building and into the parking lot.

"Myra and Joe live in a detached. Nice place," Ruth said as she veered to the west side of the parking lot where the detached condos were.

"My car is near that side. I'll walk with you."

As they neared the corner, Lexy stopped, grabbing Nans' arm to gain her attention. The other ladies halted as well. Up ahead, two men were arguing on the sidewalk in front of the entrance to one of the condos. "Who are they?"

"That one is Joe Stoddard," Ruth said. "That's their place."

"What about the other?" Nans asked. "I don't recognize him."

They ducked behind a row of shrubbery and strained to catch snippets of the men's conversation.

"—stealing my coins!" the angry guy said.

"I don't know what you're talking about," Joe Stoddard said, his tone confused.

"No switching them!" the angry man yelled at Joe. "No!"

Lexy glanced over to see Nans and the others all watching the argument as well through the leaves on the bushes. They all exchanged quizzical looks then snuck around the corner to hide behind a couple of brick pillars, the better to eavesdrop unseen from.

"These aren't the cufflinks I ordered," the angry man continued, taking a step closer to Joe and shoving his shirtsleeve into his face. "You switched the coins on me."

"I didn't. I swear," Joe said, moving back, his expression startled and his tone frazzled. "No switches."

"Why are you lying to me, Joe? The coins I gave you were valuable."

"I don't know anything about coin values. I just like to make jewelry out of them. That's it." Joe's face was flushed, and he seemed to be favoring his left side. The one where he'd had his hernia surgery, Lexy supposed. "Look, I'm sorry the cuff links didn't turn out as you'd expected. I had surgery a few weeks ago, and I'm on pain meds. Maybe they caused me to mess something up."

"That's no excuse!" the angry man snarled. "You're nothing but a liar and a cheat, using your operation as a cover for swindling people."

"I haven't swindled anyone, honest." Joe held up his hands in surrender. "All I can do is check my inventory and see if there was some kind of mix-up, okay? My wife handles inputting all that stuff into the computer, so I'll have her look this afternoon."

"Aw, poor Joe," Helen whispered from beside Lexy. "I think he's telling the truth. And he looks scared."

"There you ladies are," Myra said, coming toward them from the other side of the lot. "I've been looking for you everywhere. Are you ready to go?"

They walked toward Myra, meeting her halfway.

"Thanks for taking them where they need to go,"

Lexy yelled, remembering Myra was hard of hearing. Maybe a bit too loudly, though, judging by the way Myra jumped back. "I need to get back to work. Ladies, stop by when you're done and fill me in on what you discover."

"Will do," Nans said, waving as Lexy headed across the street to her car. "See you soon, dear."

Lexy watched them walk away, doing her best to ignore the niggle inside of her that wanted to go with them. She had a business to run and an agreement with her husband to keep. Now wasn't the time to go running off on a wild goose chase to the storage facility, no matter how intriguing it might sound.

# CHAPTER EIGHT

*a* few hours later, the lunch rush was over, and Lexy was helping Cassie clean up the tables outside when Myra's silver station wagon pulled up at the curb. The ladies climbed out, chattering like hens as they passed Lexy on their way inside to buy their daily treats.

The wind was picking up slightly, so Lexy quickly finished collecting the trash then headed inside to put the bag of refuse with the rest in the back dumpster. She joined the ladies at their table near the window after washing her hands.

"Oh, these brownies are truly divine, dear," Nans said, patting the empty seat beside her. "Sit, sit, and let us tell you what we found at Stan's."

"Personally, I prefer the pistachio biscotti," Helen

said, flicking her napkin out then laying it across her lap. "Quite tasty."

"Don't forget about these confetti cupcakes." Ida wiped a glob of vanilla frosting off her cheek. "So good."

"And what do you have, Ruth?" Lexy asked, peering across the round table at the other woman's plate.

"Today I'm trying one of those cute little peach tartlets."

"Wonderful." Lexy sipped her bottled water then rested her chin in her hand. "So were you able to get a good look at the car?"

"No," Nans said. "The police wouldn't let us through the tape, but we did get to talk with Stan again."

"Yes." Ruth swallowed a bite of her tart then shuddered. "I do wish that man would wear something over those tank tops of his. All that body hair..."

Lexy chuckled. "What did he have to say?"

"Lots. He's been paying attention whenever the cops are around, investigating." Ida devoured the last bite of her first cupcake before continuing. "According to what he's heard, the victim—Sherman Wilson—had been killed at least a few hours prior to the time we arrived. Around midnight, maybe one a.m., per what the ME said. Stan was very forthcoming with the information."

"Of course, that was before he turned all hostile with us after Ruth tried to get him to sneak us in after hours to look in her car." Helen took a dainty bite of biscotti then laid it back on her plate. With her crisp, stylish clothes and perfect silver hair, she always looked as if she was ready for the country club. No wonder the Ladies Auxiliary had practically fallen all over themselves to get Helen as a member, what with her prestigious family name around town and the old money she'd inherited from her late husband. "I've no idea what made him react so badly all of a sudden. Ruth pays a hefty price to store her car there during the winters. I don't think asking for a bit of a favor is out of the question. Especially under these circumstances."

"Well, my intuition still tells me he's hiding something," Nans said around a bite of brownie. "Didn't you hear him backtracking after we asked him about sneaking us in to see the car later tonight? He kept muttering about entrapment and telling the cops he hadn't been anywhere near that storage unit when the murder occurred and how he thought they were trying to pull something on him. Then he went off on a tangent about people wanting money from him. It was all very confusing and suspicious."

"I can tell you Stan's never been what I would call a nice man," Ruth added after finishing the last bite of her tartlet. "I've seen some pretty shady characters hanging out in the back of his office over the years. It wouldn't surprise me at all if he's doing something illegal at that storage place."

"Huh. Well, at least we managed to find out he hasn't seen any cars around that area aside from the ones we already know about." Ida popped the last of her second cupcake into her mouth then wiped her hands. "The rusted old orange Jeep, Myra's silver station wagon, and the police cars."

"Unless the person who killed Sherman Wilson didn't arrive at the storage lot by car," Lexy said before she could stop herself. Darn it. She'd vowed not to get involved. Too late now, though, considering the inquiring looks the other ladies were giving her. She shrugged and fiddled with her water bottle on the table. "I'm just saying that maybe the killer parked elsewhere and climbed the fence to get in. The killer's arrival could have all been a coincidence, and once they got there and spotted Wilson already inside, a fight ensued."

"Good point, dear." Nans smiled. "Truth is, we really just don't have enough to go on yet. Like Helen said, what we really need to find is that list. And to do that we need a way to get into Ruth's car and search inside."

Once more, the ladies turned to Lexy.

She sat back and held up her hands. "Nope. Don't look at me. I'm already in enough trouble for interfering in the case as much as I have. Besides, I promised Jack I wouldn't get involved, and I intend to keep my word. He's my husband, and we're a team too, and I need to honor that. How would it look to him if I went behind his back to sneak into a crime scene?"

"If you won't help us"—Ida glanced over at Cassie behind the counter—"then how about her?"

"Cassie? I don't know." Lexy frowned. The odd conversation they'd had about John coming home late when Jack had been relatively on time made her wary. If Cassie and John were having marital problems, the last thing Lexy wanted to do was make things worse. And John was Jack's partner on the force. What if John said something to Jack about the ladies snooping again? This sounded like a bad idea all around. "I think maybe we should—"

"Well, if you won't ask her, I will," Nans said, getting up.

Lexy asking her best friend to get her husband to let them into a restricted crime scene was bad enough. She couldn't imagine how one of the other ladies wouldn't make it worse.

"No." Lexy pushed to her feet and hurried toward the counter. "I'll do it. Hey, Cass. I hate to do this, but could you maybe ask John if he'd get us in to see Ruth's car later? I know it's still impounded, but Ruth's got a couple of things she needs to get from the vehicle, and Jack said they were done dusting for prints and swabbing for DNA."

"Oh, yeah, sure. I guess." Cassie shrugged then gave Lexy a knowing look. "What's the matter? Jack tired of you playing detective?"

*Yes.* "Sort of."

"Right." Cassie pulled out her cell phone and hit a speed dial button. Seconds later, she smiled. "Hey, John. It's me. Listen, Lexy and the ladies would like to get in to see Ruth's car later. Can you arrange that?" She grinned at Lexy, one brow raised. "Great. Yep, one hour. I'll tell her. Thanks. Oh, and if you could maybe keep this between us and not tell Jack, that'd be awesome." Her smile faltered, and she frowned down at her toes, her voice growing quieter. "No. Of course I didn't say anything. Yes, I'll let her know that, though."

Lexy's pulse stumbled. What was that about? Were Cassie and John keeping some kind of secret, or was it just her imagination? Her chest squeezed with guilt. There wasn't really much she could say about it, considering the phone call her best friend was making on her behalf, but still. The strange vibes she'd gotten from him that night with the wine and roses now took on a much more ominous tone. She waited until Cassie had ended the call then asked, "Tell me what?"

"Oh, nothing. That part wasn't about you," Cassie

slid her phone back into the pocket of her apron and avoided Lexy's gaze. "John said they're wrapping up their investigation at the scene now and they will release the vehicle in an hour."

The bells above the door jangled, and Herman Conti rushed in, making a beeline for Ruth. "Are you okay, my darling?"

Ruth harrumphed and pulled away when he tried to take her hand. "Yes, I'm fine, thank you. And I'm not your darling."

"So very glad to hear that. I've been searching you out for days," Herman continued as if Ruth weren't scowling up at him with disdain. "And what about that fine piece of automotive machinery of yours?"

"The Olds? Fine." Ruth gave him an annoyed glare. "They're releasing it from custody today."

"Ah, I see. In that case, please allow me to give you a ride, my darling." Herman made an elaborate bow, and Lexy stifled a giggle. Seemed the man was well and truly smitten with Ruth.

"It's not just me who has places to go, Herman Conti," Ruth said. "My friends and I require a ride back to my storage unit at Stan's place. Maybe you wouldn't mind driving us all?" Ruth's tone turned sweet at that last part, and she looked up at him coquettishly through her lashes.

"It would be my honor to escort you ladies anywhere you need to go," he said, gesturing to the door. "My carriage awaits at the curb, my queens."

Lexy did laugh then, not missing the eye rolls from Nans and Ida as the women stood and walked out of the bakery. A part of her couldn't help feeling a little envious, though, at all the attention Herman lavished on Ruth.

There'd been a time when she and Jack had first started dating that Jack had treated Lexy that way too. But time and familiarity had lessened their attentiveness. At least it seemed that way sometimes. Now, with overhearing Cassie's words to John, she felt even more compelled to find out what was going on with her husband. Was he bored with their life together? Was he unhappy?

"Hey, you ready to go?" Cassie asked, walking up beside Lexy.

"Huh?" Lexy gave her a confused look. "Where are we going?"

"Didn't Jack message you?"

"No." Miscommunication seemed to be the word of the day where she and her husband were concerned. "Why?"

"John said your car's done at the shop. Jack asked if I could take you over to pick it up."

"Oh." Lexy pulled out her phone to double-check, but there were no texts or missed calls. She sighed and shoved the device back into her pocket before removing her apron and grabbing her purse. Seemed she was so unimportant to Jack these days he couldn't even bother to call her himself to tell her that her car was ready, and he sent her messages via John. Not good. Not good at all.

# CHAPTER NINE

*a*fter picking up her cheery yellow VW Bug, Lexy didn't feel like going home just yet. Never mind she'd just shelled out eight hundred dollars to the mechanic, who'd claimed her baby was on its last leg. The day was sunny and warm, the breeze carried a hint of fresh pine and flowers, and she wanted to be out to experience it all. And so what if Jack hadn't bothered to call or text her all day? Jack obviously didn't see fit to tell her everything that was going on in his life, so why should she feel guilty about helping her grandmother and her friends find a menace to society, huh? She had better things to occupy her mind.

Like finding out if the ladies had discovered the whereabouts of Nunzio's mysterious list.

She signaled then pulled out into traffic and headed for the storage facility on the edge of town. With luck,

Nans and her friends would still be there, going through Ruth's Oldsmobile. Sure enough, as soon as Lexy pulled into the lot, she spotted them inside the open bay door, tearing apart the car. Parts were strewn about the ground. They might've been part of the eighty-plus crowd, but from the looks of things, the ladies could give a NASCAR pit crew a run for their money.

Lexy parked near the entrance to the storage bay and walked up to the front of the Olds, one brow raised at the sight of Ida's orthopedic shoes sticking out from beneath the vehicle's front fender, close to the same spot as the victim. She'd had no idea that any of her grandmother's friends knew anything about auto mechanics, but she'd come to expect the unexpected when it came to the Ladies Detective Club.

"Hi, ladies. Find anything interesting?" Lexy said, sidling around the tight space along the side of the car toward the back of the bay. On the opposite side of the vehicle, she spotted Ruth and Helen, busy prying off the interior door panels.

"Are you sure this is a good idea?" Helen asked Ruth. "These things don't seem to want to budge."

"Yes," Ruth said. "People hide stuff in them all the time. I saw it in a movie once."

Lexy stifled a grin and continued around to the back

of the Olds, where she found Nans with her upper body inside the trunk and her rear end jutting up in the air.

"Hey," she said, approaching slowly so as not to startle her grandmother. "What's going on?"

"Got another one!" Helen yelled from the side of the car.

"You found the list?" Lexy asked, standing on tiptoe to peer over the top of the Olds.

"What?" Helen straightened and frowned, holding up a sparkly object between her fingers. "No. Another silver dime. This thing is loaded with old change from Ruth's late husband. Must've fallen out of his pockets and into the seat cracks, I suppose. These things are rare nowadays. They don't make solid silver dimes anymore."

"True." Ruth took the coin from Helen. "I found a bunch too. In fact, that's what I had my bracelet and earrings made from as a sort of keepsake from old George." Her expression softened with nostalgia at the mention of her late husband. Old George had been gone for about forty years now, if Lexy remembered correctly.

"Did you bring us any goodies from the bakery, Lexy?" Ida asked, rolling out from beneath the car and wiping her hands on a rag, black streaks of oil and grease marring her otherwise lavender-hued hair. "I've worked up a big appetite doing this search, you know. Wouldn't want me to get weak from hunger and perish, now would you?"

"I don't think you're in danger of perishing, Ida," Nans said, removing herself from the trunk. "It hasn't been that long since our snack. Besides, we've taken this whole car apart and haven't found that blasted list."

"Obviously, Nunzio hid the list because it was dangerous. And that man was killed for it," Ruth said. "Maybe it's better that we don't find it. Maybe we *should* leave it to the police."

A brief twinge of guilt resurfaced inside Lexy over her promise to Jack. She wasn't a suspicious person by nature, but she also didn't like the idea of him keeping secrets from her. Not when he was demanding full disclosure from her. It wasn't fair. And considering she'd all but fallen off his radar these days, this small rebellion suddenly didn't seem so bad after all.

"No," she said, squaring her shoulders. "I think we should keep looking. If it's not here in the car, then the next best thing would be to find out the identity of Nunzio's associates. Maybe if we can talk to those people, we can figure out who's looking for this list and who might've killed Sherman Wilson."

"In that case, I'd say we start with Herman," Helen said. "He's sweet on Ruth, and he used to hang out a lot with Nunzio back in the day."

"He did?" Lexy was stunned. Herman Conti had seemed so sweet and honorable. But if he hung with people of Nunzio's ilk, then he couldn't have been quite so squeaky clean after all.

"Yeah, remember Ruth said Nunzio tried to warn her away from Herman because he was jealous, right?" Helen turned to Ruth.

"That's right. I guess they traveled loosely in the same circles," Ruth said.

Ida made a face. "You mean that guy with the hats used to be a gangster too? You sure know how to pick 'em."

Ruth rolled her eyes. "No, Ida. Herman wasn't a gangster. He knew Nunzio when they were young. I think maybe they worked together." Ruth scrunched her lips together and tilted her head. "Or did they go to school together?"

"Either way seems like he'd be worth talking to. We have no other leads." Lexy smiled to hide her lingering discomfort over everything. "We can go visit him tomorrow. I'll even take along a box of his favorite blueberry scones to make him more amenable to our cause."

# CHAPTER TEN

"*D*id you find anything interesting in Ruth's car?" Lexy asked Jack that night over dinner, trying to act as nonchalant as possible. It was the first time she'd talked to him all day, and her doubts from the conversation with Cassie earlier still lingered. She'd considered just coming right out and confronting him about what she'd overheard her best friend say to John, but given the current tensions between them, she didn't want to make things worse or cause a small disagreement to go into a complete meltdown. She wasn't even sure if what she'd overheard had anything to do with her. Cassie had said it didn't, and her best friend wouldn't lie, especially if it was something important about Jack.

"Honey, you know I can't really say too much about an ongoing investigation," he said around a bite of corn. He'd been quiet since he'd gotten home, which wasn't like him. He barely gave her a peck on the cheek tonight, and certainly no wine or roses. The ache in Lexy's chest intensified. "We were able to determine that the rusted-out orange Jeep on the scene belonged to the victim."

"Oh. Really?" She swallowed a bite of pork chop without really tasting it. Between the current strain on her relationship with Jack and the fact she and the ladies had found precious little in their own search of Ruth's car, that tidbit of information gave them virtually nothing to go on. "Anything else?"

Jack gave a one-shoulder shrug, still not meeting her gaze. "There was no evidence of anyone cutting the fence or breaking into the property at the storage place. The fence is pretty high and surrounds the property, so that suggests the killer came and went by car also."

Lexy perked up a bit. Now *that* was something she could work with. She snuck a tiny piece of meat to Sprinkles, who sat dutifully at her feet, then swallowed a bite of her roll and sighed. "Interesting. What about the murder weapon? Did they find any DNA from the murderer on it? Perhaps anything out of place at the crime scene?"

Jack gave her a wary look over the rim of his glass. He set it down with a decisive thump on the table and frowned. "The coroner said Wilson was killed with a small wireless drill, and the news reported that earlier.

Forensic testing of samples from the wound site showed traces of titanium from the drill bit, nothing else conclusive. Why are you asking me all these questions tonight, honey?"

"Oh, no reason." Lexy took a sip of her water, averting her gaze as her cheeks heated. A super spy she was not, apparently. Still, getting Jack annoyed was better than no response from him at all. "Just curious about your day is all. Sounds like it was pretty gruesome, with all those titanium drill bits and wound forensics."

Jack exhaled and shoved his mashed potatoes around on his plate with his fork. "That wasn't even the worst of it. The ME also said that whoever killed Wilson drilled right into his pacemaker and stopped his heart dead."

"Wow." Stunned, Lexy blinked at her husband for several seconds. "That's horrible. I didn't even know that was possible." She shook her head while cataloging the information in the back of her mind to share with the ladies later. "And you think the killer got the drill from inside Ruth's storage bay?" Lexy tried to remember the inside of the bay. It had been small, but she didn't remember a lot of tools inside. Why would Ruth have tools? Maybe they had been Nunzio's.

"That's what the evidence suggests, but my instincts say not. I'm guessing the murderer brought that weapon with them." Jack pushed his half-eaten plate of dinner away then sat back in his seat, his handsome face etched with fatigue. "Titanium drill bits are used specifically for metalworking. They're not something the ordinary person would have in their toolkit. And they aren't used on cars, unless maybe you want to drill out the VIN number to erase it."

"Huh." Lexy finished her roll then stood to clear their plates. Sprinkles followed her to the sink, glancing from the dishes to her bowl, apparently hoping Lexy would scrape some scraps into it. "Interesting. And it certainly sounds like you're right. Ruth would have no reason to have one of those lying around near her car. And she wouldn't have a need to drill out her VIN number—she owned the car."

He shrugged and shook his head. "Honestly, nothing with those ladies would surprise me anymore. Funny thing is, though, the drill we took into evidence at the crime scene wasn't the one used to kill Sherman Wilson. That drill is still missing. The only thing the one we've got was used for was to bore through the lock on the vehicle door."

"Really?" Lexy turned around at the sink and rested her hip against the edge of the counter, scowling. "What about the blood on it, though?"

Jack raised an inquisitive brow at her.

"What?" She lowered her gaze. "I saw the techs

carrying the evidence bag to the van that day is all. I'm curious."

"Hmm." His snort suggested he didn't buy that excuse for a second. Still, he thankfully let it drop. "Looks like it was just from the blood pooled on the floor from the victim, near where the drill was lying. The team's still testing it for that, though."

"Right." Lexy forced a smile and continued rinsing the plates in the sink before putting them in the dishwasher, grateful to be facing away from her husband's too-perceptive gaze. "What about fingerprints?"

"There weren't many, outside of Ruth's and Nunzio's. Based on the lint fibers found on the car's door handle, it appears our killer wore cotton gloves."

The tension in Lexy's shoulders lessened. The only other person she'd seen wearing gloves this far into summer was Ruth that day in the taxi. But hers were leather, not cotton.

As if reading her mind, Jack asked, "Didn't I see Ruth wearing a pair of white gloves that day at the crime scene?"

"What?" She fumbled a plate while sliding it into the dishwasher, barely managing to catch it before it crashed to the floor. Surely the police wouldn't suspect poor Ruth of killing that man. "No. I mean, yes. She was wearing gloves. Driving gloves. But they were leather, not cotton."

"Driving gloves sometimes have cotton fibers inside. Oh, the techs also found scattered flakes of puff pastry around the scene. Like the kind you use in your cream puffs."

The muscles between Lexy's shoulder blades knotted once more. What exactly was Jack trying to get at? Did he think the Ladies Detective Club had something to do with the killing of Sherman Wilson? Did he think Lexy did too? She glanced at him over her shoulder. The thought both annoyed and terrified her. Surely Jack knew her better than that, knew her grandmother better than that. He loved her. They loved each other. Right? "Any puff pastry you found at the scene probably came from that box of cream puffs I gave the ladies to eat while we waited for you and your team to arrive. You know how they love my baked goods. In fact, Ida had at least two that day. I saw her brush the crumbs off her top myself."

Jack's stoic façade faltered slightly under her irritated tone. A small smile quirked one side of his mouth. "All right, all right. I wasn't trying to suggest anything about Nans and the ladies. Just answering your question was all, honey. Oh, and there was one other odd thing they discovered. Near the front bumper of the car. An old buffalo nickel charm. There was a hole drilled through the top and a tiny metal hoop, like the kind you'd find on a charm bracelet. Looked like a real antique coin too."

"Huh." Lexy finished loading the dishwasher then turned to wipe down the table. "I'll save you some detective work then and let you know that Ruth has a charm bracelet like that. She just had it made, actually, using coins she found inside the Olds. She was wearing it the morning we went to pick up her car, and the clasp broke. When she went to pick it up off the ground is when she discovered Sherman Wilson's body and—" Lexy stopped at Jack's narrowed stare. "What?"

"You don't find it odd that her bracelet just happened to break at the exact place where a dead body was stashed?"

Indignation flared inside Lexy. What was he trying to say? He had some nerve implying Ruth's bracelet getting caught wasn't just an accident, especially with the way he'd been acting all weird lately. Without thinking, she blurted out, "Nice of you to let me know my car was ready earlier."

Jack wrinkled his nose. "What are you talking about, honey?"

"Obviously, you were too busy finding ways to implicate my grandmother and her friends to call or text me yourself."

"Wait a minute." Jack held his hands up in defense.

"You're mad because I had John relay the message through Cassie? I was just trying to be efficient is all. Since Cassie already had him on the line, I thought it would save time to just have her tell you. And since it was close to quitting time at the bakery, I figured you could catch a ride to the body shop with her."

Arms crossed, Lexy frowned. When he put it that way, it sounded downright logical. Which only served to irk her more. She tried never to be a drama queen, but right now, she felt confused and vulnerable and completely discombobulated, and she didn't like it one bit.

She grasped the end of her long mink-brown ponytail, which hung over her shoulder, toying with it absently. Jack remained silent, his expression cautious as he watched her as if she were a ticking time bomb ready to explode.

Even Sprinkles seemed to pick up on the tension curdling in the air between them. She whimpered and ran to her dog bed in the corner.

To defuse the situation, Lexy forced herself to take a deep breath then refocused on her friend's defense. "You can't honestly think Ruth had anything to do with that man's murder, Jack. You know her. She wouldn't hurt a flea. None of the ladies would."

"I suppose not," Jack said after a beat. "And it does

seem hard to picture a woman of Ruth's age able to open that storage bay door without assistance."

Lexy refrained from saying that she'd seen Ruth do that very thing with ease. That certainly wouldn't help Ruth at all at this point. Instead, she dried her hands on a nearby dishtowel and chuckled, the sound nervous and stilted even to her own ears. "True. And then there's the fact she has no motive either."

"That we know about," Jack said cryptically.

"Seriously?" Lexy said, exasperated. "Why in the world would Ruth kill that man then volunteer to return first thing in the morning with a bunch of witnesses?"

"No one would expect it," Jack said. "Most killers would avoid the place. Sounds pretty clever to me. And those ladies are nothing if not clever."

Not giving up so easily, Lexy continued to plead Ruth's case. "You said the lock was cut. Ruth wouldn't have to do that. She had the key."

"Maybe Wilson cut the lock before she got there."

"Honestly, Jack. You need to stop. Ruth's our friend, not a suspect in your case."

He snorted and stood, stretching before walking over and sliding his arms around Lexy's waist, pulling her stiff form against him. "Well, she has been known to cavort with criminals, after all. Nunzio Bartolli wasn't exactly a choirboy."

"No." She sighed, her husband's warmth melting her resistance, despite her wishes to the contrary. Unable to resist, she slid her palms up his chest and met his gaze, not missing the twinkle in his eye. He was teasing her, darn him. They'd been married long enough to know which buttons to push on the other for maximum effect. Both a blessing and a curse.

Jack broke into a full-blown grin, and his good humor was infectious. Soon, Lexy found herself smiling back at him, her suspicions and hurt from earlier buried beneath an avalanche of affection. She gave a small shrug. "I guess you're right."

"I'm sorry. Could you repeat that please?"

"What?"

"The 'you're right' part. I hear it so rarely these days."

She gave him a look, and Jack laughed and pulled Lexy into a tight hug. "Sorry, honey. I couldn't resist getting you going a bit. And I'm sorry about not calling you myself earlier today about your car. It was an honest, if stupid, mistake. I didn't think anything of it and never meant to upset you. Please forgive me?"

She buried her nose in his neck, loving the musky, woodsy scent of his aftershave. When she was in Jack's arms, she'd forgive him nearly anything. *He's hiding something.* She shoved the traitorous thought deep and clung tighter to her husband. Jack was here. Jack had apologized. Jack loved her, and she loved him. Everything was fine. "You're forgiven."

"Thank you, honey. Oh, and tell Ruth when you see her tomorrow that she needs an oil change." Jack kissed the top of her head then pulled back slightly to meet her gaze. "Okay?"

"Okay. But what makes you think I'm going to see her tomorrow?" she said, smiling.

Jack gave her a quick kiss on the lips then pulled away. "Because I know you, and I know the ladies. Just promise me you'll be careful and that you'll call me if you get into any sticky situations, all right?"

Lexy trailed after him toward the living room, the warmth of familiarity swelling inside her. It wasn't exactly a blessing on her snooping, but she'd take it. The niggle of doubt inside her reared its ugly head one last time. *Maybe he's giving you freedom so you won't poke into his business.* But as they snuggled on the sofa in the living room, she felt safe and protected in his arms, and for tonight, at least, all was right with their little world.

# CHAPTER ELEVEN

The next day, Lexy was happy to drive herself to work in her VW. No more bumming rides. She had her car back, and they'd even detailed the inside and put one of those new-car-smell air fresheners in. It wasn't as good as the real new-car smell, but it had been so long since Lexy actually had a new car she barely noticed the difference.

She ignored the slight bucking at the stoplight and the whirring sound coming from the engine as she pulled into the alley behind the bakery. They'd replaced a lot of things in the car, so strange sounds were probably normal, right?

The morning was a little slow, and Lexy handled the usual rush of morning-commute customers who wanted to grab a coffee and pastry before work with ease. She stocked up the self-serve coffee area and mixed up some cake batter and baked three pans of cake for a triple-decker birthday cake someone had ordered. When things slowed down, she took off her yellow gingham apron and hung it on the rack.

"I'm heading over to Nans' for a bit," Lexy said to Cassie. "Will you be okay here by yourself for a few hours?"

"Yes, I'll be fine," Cassie said. "We haven't had any customers in an hour. I'll probably go in the back and begin working on the list of items to make for tomorrow. I can pop out front if someone comes in."

"Okay." Lexy finished tying a bow in the pink-and-white-striped twine binding the box of fresh almond scones she'd packed. Given his penchant for them the other day, she thought they were Herman Conti's favorite, and she didn't want to disappoint, especially today, when they hoped to grill him for information. "I'll see you later then."

"See ya." Cassie waved as Lexy headed out into the bright afternoon sunshine. The warm air, full of the scent of freshly mown grass, felt refreshing on her skin. She stopped at her car to unlock the doors and smiled at the low burble of the waterfall nearby. Last night had gone a long way toward easing her fears about her marriage and Jack. After their tiff after dinner, they'd seemed much more in sync again. Enough so that he'd even given his half-hearted assent to her meeting with the ladies, which was good because, from what Nans had said at her condo yesterday, they had no intention of not investigating the murder of Sherman Wilson.

She climbed behind the wheel of the Bug and started the engine. It still wheezed and sputtered a bit, but it was better than before, and the traffic was light this midafternoon. Within five minutes, she was knocking on Nans' door.

"Finally, you're here," her grandmother said, answering. "Ida's been waiting for the pastry."

Lexy followed Nans into the condo, finding Ruth, Ida, and Helen seated at Nans' mahogany table. Each lady had a dainty porcelain cup nestled in its matching saucer on the table in front of them.

"Oh, she's here!" Ida darted up from her seat and ran to Lexy, lifting the corner of the pastry box from the side to peek in without disturbing the twine tying it shut.

"Those are for Herman," Ruth admonished her, smacking her hand away. "At least wait until we are at his house."

"Well, he can't eat the whole box." Ida dispensed with politeness completely then and opened the box, grabbing the largest of the scones. "See? There's plenty here for everyone. Even your precious Herman."

As Ida scarfed down the scone and the others took

their teacups into the kitchen, Nans said, "We're almost ready to go, dear, but we need to discuss how we are going to get Herman to talk."

"I think our best bet is for Ruth to charm him," Helen said as she carefully dried a dainty teacup with tiny cornflower blue flowers around the rim.

"Yeah," Ida agreed. "Maybe you should go alone, Ruth. That way you can put the moves on him. He'll be more eager to spill his guts if you persuade him the right way." Ida waggled her brows. "If you know what I mean."

"That might not be a good idea," Nans cautioned. "Herman knew Nunzio, and Nunzio even warned Ruth about him. What if that warning had nothing to do with jealousy? What if Herman is one of Nunzio's "associates"? Herman could be on the list. He could even be the killer."

"That's ridiculous," Ruth said. "Herman and Nunzio hated each other. They wouldn't have been associates."

"I don't know, Nans," Lexy agreed. "Herman seems awfully nice."

"Of course he is. I'm sure Nunzio was just jealous," Helen said. "Herman Conti couldn't hurt a flea. But I think we should all go and talk to him. We wouldn't want Ruth to have all the fun, and besides, it's better if all of us hear what he has to say. Each one of us might have a different take on it."

"Okay, then what are we waiting for?" Ida brushed past them on her way to the door. "Lexy, you can fill us in on anything you learned from Jack on the way out."

As Nans locked up, Lexy brought them up to speed on what Jack told her the night before. "Oh, and they have the charm for your bracelet, Ruth."

Ruth's hand flew to her naked wrist, her brow furrowed. "My bracelet?"

"Maybe it came off when the clasp broke," Ida suggested. "That's how you found the body, remember?"

"Of course I remember," Ruth said, her expression odd. "One doesn't forget such an awful sight, Ida."

Lexy followed the ladies through the hall, into the elevator, and out to the parking lot. They hustled over to Lexy's VW Bug, walking right past Ruth's car.

"You got the Olds from the storage place already? Maybe we should take that instead." She pointed at the large blue vehicle. "There'd be a lot more room."

"Can't," Helen said. "The door panels are still off inside."

"We didn't have time to put it all back together, and Stan said we had to get it out of the storage bay, so we drove it like it was," Ruth said. "It wasn't a comfortable ride."

"Oh." Lexy turned to peer into the car. The ladies were right. The interior of the Olds was a mess after all the ladies digging through it plus the police investigation. It would take some serious detailing to get it back into shape again.

"That's strange," Nans said, scowling. "I would've sworn we'd laid those door panels on the backseat, but now they're on the floor."

"Do you think someone was in there, rifling around?" Lexy asked as they all piled into her VW. The Bug wasn't really built to accommodate all those people, but the ladies were used to creatively squeezing themselves into all sorts of tight places, and they somehow managed to fit Ruth, Ida and Helen into the backseat with Nans riding shotgun. Lexy buckled her seatbelt and started the engine, her cheeks heating when the VW backfired loudly as they headed out of the parking lot.

Ruth scooted in her seat a bit, jostling Ida, who gave her an annoyed stare. "Doesn't matter anyway. If someone else *was* looking for something in the Olds, they won't find anything."

"Ouch," Helen said, shooting Ida a scowl. "You kicked me."

"Sorry." Ida shrugged and grinned. "It's tight back here."

"Take a left," Ruth commanded. "Next right, then all the way to the end."

Lexy followed her directions, and soon they were

parked    before    a    majestic-looking    old
Victorian-style home.

Herman answered the door, his eyes lighting up
when they fell on Ruth then darkening when he saw that
she had company. "I didn't realize you were all coming."

"I needed Lexy to drive me, and then the others just
tagged along." Ruth breezed into the foyer, and Lexy and
the other ladies followed.

"Oh, that's right. Your car is out of commission,"
Herman said as he closed the door. "Err... I mean it must
still be impounded by the police."

"I got it back. But it's not exactly drivable." Ruth took
the bakery box from Lexy. "We brought some scones.
Should we go in the kitchen?"

"Certainly." Herman half bowed and indicated for
them to proceed down a hallway with golden oak wood
that smelled like lemons and into an airy kitchen that
boasted Paris-blue cabinets, slate flooring, and a long
pine trestle table. If nothing else, Herman had good taste.
And a lot of money, considering the expensive furniture
and antiques, not to mention the Waterford crystal
platter he was transferring the scones onto.

They sat down at the table, and Lexy dipped her tea
bag into the steaming water in her cup. She picked a
scone up off the tray and nibbled while Herman compli-
mented each of the ladies in turn. Ruth's outfit, Nans'

hair, Helen's shoes, Ida's complexion. He was quite the ladies' man.

"The police don't seem to be making much headway on the murder investigation," Nans said out of the blue.

Herman's cup rattled as he placed it a little too forcefully in the saucer. "That's a shame. Nasty business. I hate to think of a killer running loose." He turned to Ruth. "Would you like another scone?"

Ruth's brows mashed together as she looked at her plate, where she still had three-quarters of her scone left. "No thanks."

"Anyone for more tea?" Herman got up to heat more water.

Lexy stretched. She didn't want more tea, and this conversation seemed to be going nowhere. Herman hadn't taken the bait about the murder, and now Nans and Ruth were giving each other raised-eyebrow looks and head jerks as they silently tried to tell each other to continue questioning.

"So were you good friends with Nunzio Bartolli?" Nans blurted out. "Ruth dated him, you know."

Herman's brow furrowed. The teakettle whistled, and he turned around, shutting off the burner and grabbing the kettle. "I knew him peripherally. I wouldn't say we were friends."

Herman came back to the table with the teapot and started pouring.

"No more tea for me." Lexy put her hand over her cup. "You have beautiful antiques here."

Herman's face brightened. "Thank you. Been collecting for years. Have a look around."

Lexy made her way into the dining room beside the kitchen. The room was painted a lovely muted blue, which complemented the gold-and-cobalt oriental rug that sat under the oak oval claw-foot table. On one wall was an oak china cabinet to match, the sides boasting curved glass doors that looked to be the original wavy glass. Inside, a display of crystal vases sparkled.

The wall opposite the china cabinet was covered in old photographs displayed in lavish gilt frames. Studying the pictures, Lexy found herself enchanted by the views of her beloved Brook Ridge Falls in earlier times. Most of the faces she didn't recognize, but a few looked familiar.

She squinted and leaned in closer to inspect the photo in front of her. It showed some kind of club in the background and a group of men in suits near the front. They all looked to be in their midtwenties and were all smiling and laughing, their arms around each other's shoulders. "These shots are really interesting."

"Yes, they bring back a lot of memories..." Ruth peered at the same photo as Lexy, frowning. She spun away fast, obviously flustered, and made a show of checking her watch. "Oh, look at the time! I forgot all about my hair appointment today, and I need to leave immediately or miss it entirely."

Confused, Lexy followed Ruth into the kitchen, where Ruth grabbed Ida by the elbow and explained to Nans and Herman about the hair appointment.

"I'm so sorry." Ruth patted at the top of her head. "But I simply cannot miss the appointment."

"But you can't leave yet. You just got here," Herman said, his tone disappointed. "I didn't even have a chance to invite you to the early-bird dinner at The Millhouse, Ruth."

"I'm sorry," Ruth said, packing up a scone and stuffing it in her purse. "I'll have to get back to you on that, Herman."

Ruth swept them all toward the front door. As they bid hasty good-byes to Herman, Ruth broke from the crowd and made a beeline for the car.

"What in the world was that all about?" Nans asked as she and Lexy got into the front seats.

"Not sure. We were looking at old photos in the dining room, and Ruth suddenly panicked and—"

"I did not panic," Ruth said from the backseat, where she was already sitting with her hands clenched. "I was shocked. That's all. That photo we were looking at,

Lexy." She glanced back toward Herman's house. "I recognized the location. It was Nunzio's old headquarters in Cold Springs. And Herman was there, with that group of men. I'm afraid he *is* involved with organized crime."

"Seriously?" Ida gaped as she wedged her way into the middle of the back seat.

"I don't know," Lexy said, starting up the car. "He seems like such a sweet old man."

"Hmm. I'm sure Al Capone would've seemed sweet too, had he lived to a ripe old age," Nans said, snorting.

"It *was* kind of odd the way he mentioned Ruth's vehicle today," Helen said. "Perhaps he wasn't so concerned about courting Ruth all this time and was looking for something else instead. Do you think it might have been Herman who was poking around inside the Olds?"

"Could be," Ruth said. "He knew I was out yesterday morning."

"Maybe he is the killer?" Ida suggested.

"More research. That's what we need." Nans twisted around to look at the backseat. "Helen?"

Lexy glanced in the rearview to see Helen pulling an iPad out of her oversized patent-leather purse.

"I'm on it," Helen said.

The car was filled with the sound of clacking keys.

"Looks like we have a hit. An old newspaper article," Ruth said. "Says here that he and Nunzio were linked to a liquor store robbery back when they were teenagers. Of course, that was sixty-five years ago, but it shows he was into crime with Nunzio. He could be one of the guys on Nunzio's list."

"And if he knew Ruth was out yesterday, that gave him opportunity to search her Olds," Helen said.

"Does anyone know where he was when Wilson was killed?" Nans asked.

They all shook their heads.

"Did he know you stored the Olds at Stan's, Ruth?" Ida asked.

"I'm not sure," Ruth said.

"He *might* have had motive, he certainly has means because, even though he's old, it wouldn't be too hard to kill someone by jamming a drill into their pacemaker, and he might have had opportunity." Ida's eyes sparkled. "Looks like we better tell Jack."

# CHAPTER TWELVE

The Brook Ridge Falls police station was in a low brick building. It wasn't anything fancy, with an industrial tile lobby and plastic chairs. Inside, the air conditioning whooshed, computer keys clacked, and a bored-looking teenager slouched in one of the chairs.

"Hi, I'm here to see my husband, Jack," Lexy said to the receptionist. The gal had been working at the station as long as Lexy could remember and looked more like a librarian than a desk clerk, with her horn-rimmed glasses and schoolmarm expression. Lexy flashed her brightest smile, hoping to gain the woman's favor. "Is he available?"

"Let me check," the receptionist said, picking up her phone. Lexy glanced around at the scattered paperwork atop the woman's desk as she waited. Several traffic citations and a damage-to-public-property report but nothing about the Sherman Wilson case, unfortunately. The receptionist hung up and sighed. "I'm sorry. Jack's with someone right now. May I give him a message?"

"No, thanks. I'll wait." Lexy returned to where the ladies were sitting against the far wall of the lobby, looking like some kind of geriatric crime-fighting brigade, with their massive patent-leather bags lined up across their laps and their postures prim. It had been a while since she'd visited Jack at work. The station still looked the same—same yellowing linoleum floor, same fluorescent bulbs buzzing overhead, same hum of activity from the back room, where all the action took place. Feeling antsy, Lexy glanced back at the restroom near the gate into the back area, an idea occurring. She smiled down at Nans. "I'm going to use the restroom. Be right back."

"Sure," Nans said, looking over to see where it was located then back to Lexy, her gaze knowing. "Fine, dear. Perhaps I'll go with you."

"Actually, I was hoping you could watch my things."

"Oh. Of course, dear."

Lexy handed her purse to Nans then headed for the bathroom, double-checking to make sure the receptionist was otherwise occupied. Then, as she passed the gate leading to the back offices, she made a quick detour down the hall and peeked around the corner into Jack's office.

Her smile fell fast, and her heart sank. He was busy, all right—with an attractive blonde. Given the way she was leaning over Jack's arm and all but shoving her cleavage in his face, the pair looked quite chummy at the moment. Cheeks hot and mind racing, she hurried back down the hall to the bathroom. *He's having an affair. Jack's having an affair. That's his big secret.*

That was what Cassie and John had tried to keep hidden from her.

At first, she felt numb. This couldn't be happening. Not to her. Not to Jack. Not to their marriage. They'd been so happy, so in love. He'd brought her flowers and wine just the other night, for goodness' sake.

Then the numbness gave way to anger and then to tears.

She sat in the stall, alone, and cried silently for several minutes.

Finally, all cried out, resignation set in.

If Jack was cheating on her, what was she going to do about it? Roll over and let the other woman steal the love of her life? Not likely. She wasn't Nans' granddaughter for nothing.

She'd fight. That was what she'd do. Fight to keep Jack and fight to keep their marriage alive. But first, she needed to scope out her opponent. See what she was up against. Yep.

Lexy Baker refused to go down without a fight.

By the time she came out again, she felt a bit more in

control of her emotions, if not her thoughts. Maybe she was overreacting. Jack and the blonde weren't actually *doing* anything to suggest an affair, and she could hardly expect him to deal with only male colleagues or criminals. She shouldn't jump to conclusions. But just in case, she was going to keep a close eye out.

Before she got herself all worked up again, Lexy walked over to where the ladies were sitting in the lobby and slumped down into an empty seat.

"Everything all right, dear?" Nans asked, her tone concerned as she passed Lexy's purse back to her.

"Yes, I—"

Her response was cut off by Jack walking into the lobby, the blonde by his side. They were both smiling and laughing, just as he and Lexy used to do together. He didn't look away from his companion, so chances were good he had no idea his wife was watching him. Just in case, she scooted down in her chair and picked up one of the dog-eared magazines from the table beside her to hold in front of her face. Which, honestly, was stupid, considering the rest of the ladies were sitting right beside her in plain sight.

"I'll call you later tonight," Jack said to the blonde as he held the door for her. He was whistling—*actually whistling*, as if life was grand—when he turned around and stopped short. "Mona? Is that you? What are you ladies doing here?" Lexy winced as his finger slowly tipped her magazine down so she could meet his gaze. "With my wife?"

Slowly, she straightened in her seat and tried to pretend everything was fine. "Hi, Jack."

He crossed his arms and narrowed his gaze. "What's going on?"

She wanted to ask him the same question about the blonde who'd just left, but refrained. What would she say, anyway? *Is this your new girlfriend? My replacement?* No, she must be overreacting, because Jack wouldn't be standing there all calm, cool, and collected if he'd just ushered his girlfriend out. Would he?

She pushed to her feet and slung her bag over her shoulder, forcing a confident smile she didn't quite feel. "We may know who killed Sherman Wilson."

Jack exhaled slowly, his tense shoulders relaxing slightly as he waved the ladies back into the main area of the station. "Come on back to my office, where we can talk privately."

As usual, it was a tight squeeze fitting all of them inside the small room, but Jack managed to somehow get the door closed then took a seat behind his desk. "Okay. What do you ladies have for me?"

"The gentleman's name is Herman Conti. He's an old friend of Ruth *and* Nunzio Bartolli's, and he seems like the most likely suspect at this point," Nans said. "We've Googled him and have discovered he's got a criminal background and motive."

"What motive?" Jack looked incredulous. "And since when do you know how to surf the Internet, Mona?"

"Oh, it wasn't me, Jack. It was Helen."

Helen waved from the corner.

Nans continued. "Mr. Conti's motive, we believe, is to keep his nefarious past hidden."

"I don't know." Jack scrubbed a hand over his face then fixed Lexy with a pointed stare. "Didn't we discuss not investigating any more of these murders on your own?"

Indignation prickled Lexy's cheeks with heat. "Last night, you gave me your blessing to see the ladies again today. What did you think we were going to do, Jack? Play bridge all day? Besides, Nans needed help."

*Like you were helping yourself to that blonde.* She bit back those words, barely.

"She's right. It's my fault," Nans said. "I asked Lexy to drive us over to Herman's today. She was only being a good granddaughter. But it was there that we saw proof of Mr. Conti's connection to the crime."

"Really?" Jack gave his wife some serious side-eye. "And what might that be?"

"A photo," Lexy said, crossing her arms. "It showed

Nunzio and Herman Conti together, hanging out when they were younger."

"And don't forget the Internet search," Helen said. "Turns out the two of them robbed a bank together years ago. Both served time for it too."

"Take a look for yourself." Ruth pulled the iPad out of her huge handbag and turned on the screen then handed it to Jack. "And Herman knew I wouldn't be home yesterday morning when my condo was broken into because he'd asked me to brunch, but I turned him down because I was busy."

Jack shook his head and snorted. "Let me get this straight. You ladies want me to arrest this guy because he committed a crime over sixty years ago and asked Ruth out for brunch?"

"Well, when you put it that way, it does sound a little far-fetched, but we're certain it's him," Helen said, squaring her shoulders. "And you should've seen how squirrelly he got when we brought up the murder to him earlier. Plus, he kept asking about Ruth's car. When we walked by it this afternoon, the door panels on the back-seat had been moved. I wouldn't be surprised at all if he'd broken into her Olds to search it."

"Or maybe"—Jack tapped the screen a few times then chuckled—"he was rattled because you ladies have suddenly become social media stars." He handed the iPad back to Ruth. "Pictures of you all tearing apart the Oldsmobile in that storage bay are all over the Internet. People have dubbed you guys the Silver Sensations."

"Really?" the ladies said in unison.

Ida grabbed the iPad from Jack and scrolled through the photos. Lexy leaned over her shoulder in time to see several unflattering photos of the ladies—Nans with her hind end sticking out of the trunk, Ruth and Helen arguing over a coin, the toes of Ida's orthopedic shoes pointing out from beneath the fender of the Olds.

"Darn," Ida said. "That's not my best angle."

"None of these are flattering." Nans shook her head. "Who could've taken them?"

"Probably Rena Gulch. She's had it in for us since day one." Helen gave a dismissive wave.

"Oh, this is just terrible." Ruth sighed. "Look at those awful images. Whoever took them made sure to angle the shots to make us look fat."

Nans pointed to one, her expression aghast. "Is my butt really that big?"

Jack gave a long-suffering sigh then stood and opened his office door. "Ladies, I hate to cut this short, but I need to get back to work. Is there anything else I can help you with?"

"Are you at least going to bring Herman in to question him?" Lexy asked, bristling under his dismissal. How dare he treat them like a bunch of silly busybodies? She was still his wife. She deserved more respect.

"I doubt it, honey." Jack ushered them all back out to the hallway. "I'd need a lot more than what you've given me to bring him in."

He reached for her arm and leaned in to kiss her goodbye, but Lexy shook him off. The trouble between them right now would take more than a couple endearments and kisses to fix. "What do you need then?"

"Proof. A confession." Jack frowned at her. "Is something wrong, honey?"

"No." Yes. She looked away, not wanting him to see the doubt in her eye. "We'll get out of your hair, for now. Will you be home for dinner tonight?" *Or will you be seeing the blonde?*

"I'll be home at my regular time, honey. See you then."

Nans glanced between the two of them then shook her head. "You should listen to me more often, Jack. I'm usually right. But if you say you need more evidence to bring Herman Conti in, then we'll just get him to confess to the murder. And I know exactly how to do it."

CHAPTER THIRTEEN

*L*exy dropped the ladies off at their retirement community to weave their plans then headed back to The Cup and Cake. She still needed to balance the receipts from the day before and help Cassie finish making the goodies for the next day. She stopped at a red light then winced as the Bug sputtered and bucked hard once more. The mechanic had warned her it wouldn't last long even with his latest intervention, but her baby had sentimental value, and she didn't want to believe it. She'd had the Bug since she'd first opened the bakery. It was the vehicle she'd driven the day she'd first met Jack and the same one she'd used to cart Nans and the ladies around for all their sleuthing. Heck, it was almost an honorary member of the Ladies Detective Club.

By the time Lexy reached the shop and got her purse

stowed and her receipts settled, Cassie was done with the croissants and éclairs and was starting the dough for the cream puffs. Today, Lexy chose a frilly pink apron with tiny strawberries and hearts embroidered on it then headed back into the kitchen to help Cassie.

"Hey," Lexy said, washing her hands in the sink. "How's it going here?"

"Still slow. But I've used the downtime wisely. Got most of the stuff for tomorrow done except for these," Cassie said, spooning the pâte à choux dough into a pastry bag for piping onto the baking sheet. "How'd things go with Nans?"

"Fine." Lexy frowned as she dried her hands then slipped on a pair of gloves.

"Really?" Cassie glanced up at her. "You don't look like everything is fine."

"I'm fine. Really. Everything's great. Now, let me get to work so I can help you." Lexy prepared her own bag of dough then squirted it out onto another parchment-lined baking sheet in perfect little rounds. Baking always took her to her Zen place, and she'd never been more grateful for that than she was today. Her head was starting to ache from all the stress, right along with her heart.

"All righty then," Cassie said, focusing on her tray of dough instead. "Did they like the scones?"

"Yep. Ida ate two as usual." Lexy squinted at her tray,

willing her shaking hands to steady so she wouldn't mess up her perfect circles.

"What else did you do? Anything exciting?"

"The ladies and I stopped to see Jack at the station." The words felt like sharp glass in her throat, and Lexy swallowed hard.

"Yeah?" Cassie's hand slipped, squirting dough in an uneven squiggle across her baking sheet. She mumbled a curse and grabbed a piece of paper towel to carefully wipe up the tiny mess. Lexy didn't miss the hint of guilt that crept across her best friend's face. From what Lexy had heard of her phone call with John the other day, Cassie had known about Jack keeping secrets from Lexy. But did she know about the blonde too? Lexy intended to find out.

"What did he have to say?" Cassie asked, the tightness in her voice at direct odds with her sunny smile.

Lexy narrowed her gaze on Cassie. "Not much. He was busy, so we only got to see him for a few minutes. He was busy with someone when we first got there."

"Huh." Cassie finished her tray then began a second one, working faster than Lexy had ever seen her. "Well, busy is good, I guess."

"Hmm." Lexy double-checked the ovens to make sure they were set at 375 degrees then whisked together eggs and water to make an egg wash to brush over the tops. As she went down the line, she smoothed the top of each puff with her finger before brushing the egg mixture on top to ensure an even rise. "Do you know anything about a new blonde working at the station? Perhaps helping Jack and John on a case?"

Cassie froze for a second before continuing to pipe the last tray of pastry dough, and the nervous knots in Lexy's stomach only tightened. What was Cassie not telling her? Part of Lexy wanted to just come out and blurt what she'd seen, to confide in her best friend and hash out a plan to win her husband back. But the other part of her felt embarrassed and scared and ashamed of what was going on. And until she had concrete proof that Jack really did have something going on with the blonde, she didn't want to let the cracks show. She could be wrong.

"Oh, gosh. They work with so many people, it's hard to keep track," Cassie said, her tone vague as she squirted out the last of the dough then took the empty mixing bowl and pastry bags to the sink. "Was that who you saw with Jack today? A blonde?"

Lexy transferred the baking sheets to the ovens then set the timer for thirty minutes. They'd bake the puffs today then let them cool overnight before filling them with cream first thing in the morning to keep them fresh for the customers.

Back in high school, there'd been a boy Lexy had dated who'd ran around on her with one of the cheerleaders behind Lexy's back. At the time, Cassie had been ready to throttle the guy. Yet her reaction now, when Lexy mentioned the blonde, was only mild interest at best, and it made Lexy doubt herself once more.

Could she be blowing this whole thing with the blonde out of proportion?

Cassie was her best friend. Surely she'd tell Lexy if something bad was going on between that blonde and Jack, right? This couldn't be the secret she'd whispered about to John right in front of Lexy the other day. Nobody would be that cruel, would they? She put her hands on her hips and tapped her toe on the hardwood floor.

Unless John and Jack were in cahoots and had sworn Cassie to secrecy...

No. Cassie was loyal to Lexy. She wouldn't keep this kind of secret even if her own husband wanted her to.

In the end, she decided to let the matter drop for now, focusing instead on handling the after-school rush of moms picking up treats for their kids' sports teams and practices.

About three o'clock, Lexy's phone buzzed in the pocket of her apron, and she pulled it out to see a message from Jack, and the lump in her throat formed anew. Suddenly, he had to work late again. Stuck at the station, interviewing suspects, he said. When only hours earlier, he'd promised to be home for dinner. He must've only said that because she'd put him on the spot in front of all the ladies. If he was going to call the blonde later as he'd said, then most likely he'd never planned to come home at all.

The last thing she wanted was to sit home alone with Sprinkles, in their empty house, and wait for Jack to show up. She considered going back to Nans', but the last line of Jack's text was specific—*stay home and don't get involved in any more of your grandmother's shenanigans.*

Fresh anger welled up inside her. How dare he tell her what she could and couldn't do when he was out gallivanting around with some strange blonde, doing who knew what?

She'd go home, feed Sprinkles, and let her out to potty, then she'd pamper herself.

Maybe a manicure and pedicure, perhaps a facial and a massage to go along with it.

Yep. That sounded like a fine plan.

But after they locked the doors at five thirty, Lexy felt tired clear to her bones. Maybe it was the busy day, or maybe it was all the extra anxiety of worrying about Jack and his mysterious blonde. She took off her apron and reached for her purse beneath the counter, only to have her phone buzz again.

Perhaps Jack had reconsidered and was coming home on time after all. More eagerly than she wanted, Lexy pulled out her phone.

No such luck.

It was Nans. She and the ladies had a plan and were putting it in place to trap Herman Conti into a recorded confession. She wanted Lexy to be part of it. Even with all that had happened today, going against Jack's wishes still sat wrong with Lexy. But the hurt and anger brewing inside her soon overrode everything else.

"I'm out of here," Cassie called from the back. "See you in the morning?"

"I'll be here," Lexy murmured, distracted.

"Are you sure you're all right?" Cassie asked, her expression concerned.

"What?" Lexy looked up, forcing a smile. "Yes. I'm fine. Great. Have a good night."

She closed up then got in her Bug and headed for home to let the dog out before she went to meet the ladies.

# CHAPTER FOURTEEN

The Millhouse was an upscale restaurant in an old paper mill on the outskirts of Brook Ridge Falls. Lexy hadn't been there in ages, but the moment she stepped inside, the ambiance struck her again. Wide pine floors, stone walls, exposed beams in the high ceilings. She caught a whiff of steak, and her stomach growled almost loud enough to be heard over the hushed tones of the diners and the subtle clink of cutlery against porcelain. The space radiated warmth and luxury and the easy elegance of a time gone by. With its many hidden alcoves and booths tucked into corners, it was also quite romantic.

She spotted Nans, Helen, and Ida at a table near the windows overlooking the pond beside the restaurant. Across the room sat Ruth and Herman. Part of Nans' plan had involved Ruth accepting his invitation to early-bird dinner. Now, the ladies spied on them from behind a potted plant near their table.

As discreetly as possible, Lexy hurried over to the ladies' table and sat down, hoping to avoid being seen by Herman. She greeted everyone then peered through the leaves of the ficus to see Ruth and their suspect beyond.

"Aw, they look sweet together," Lexy said. Even with everything they'd learned about Herman Conti's past, she still had a hard time picturing the old charmer as a hardened criminal. Then again, she'd had a hard time picturing her husband straying too. Seemed her radar where the opposite sex was concerned was way off. She opened her menu and tried to concentrate on the specials of the day instead of her marital issues.

"We'll see how cute he is when he's drunk," Nans said, perusing her menu as well.

"Drunk?" Lexy said, staring at her grandmother.

"Yes, that's the plan, dear. Ruth is going to get him liquored up, loosening his tongue, and then we'll get him to confess." She tapped her phone, which was set in the middle of their table with the speaker turned on. "Helen was able to download an app that acts like a recorder to Ruth's phone. All I have to do is dial her number, and we're connected to their conversation."

The waitress came and took their orders then brought their drinks—white wine for Lexy, tea for the ladies. Once the server left, Nans dialed Ruth's number then placed the phone back into the center of the table, and they all leaned forward to listen.

"Let me get you another drink, Herman," Ruth said over the phone line.

"Ohr, no, my durling. I'm gurd," Herman said, already slurring his words a bit. "I think some furd is in order. Don't wanna get sloshed on our first date." He chuckled a little longer and louder than appropriate.

Ruth gave a decidedly annoyed sigh. "Why don't you try your steak then? How is it?"

"Delicious," Herman said, chewing loudly. "How's yur pasta?"

"Fine."

Through the plants, Lexy spotted Ruth staring at the table, her expression frustrated. Seemed their plan wasn't going as smoothly as they'd expected. Finally, Ruth sat back and dabbed her mouth with a linen napkin. "You and my Nunzio weren't always enemies, were you?"

"What?" Herman scowled. "N-No."

"He mentioned you, you know," Ruth said.

From beside Lexy, Nans grinned and nodded toward the phone. "Here we go."

"He did?" Herman's voice sounded a bit shakier now. "I can't imagine why."

"Perhaps it was because of his place at Cold Springs. I saw the picture of you two there on your wall earlier."

Herman snorted. "One photo doesn't prove anything."

"Yes." A shuffling noise issued as Ruth shifted in her seat, suggesting her cell phone was hidden in her pocket. "The victim they found under my car in the storage bay. His name was Sherman Wilson. He was from Cold Springs too, if I'm not mistaken. Did you know him too, Herman...?"

Ruth's voice trailed off.

"Wilson? Hmm," Herman said, his tone growing a tad agitated. "Nope, never heard of 'im."

"Why are you getting upset?" Ruth asked. "Do you have something to hide?"

"Hide? Me? Nah." Herman gave a nervous laugh. "What're you trying to say, my durrling?"

"Nothing. It's just that my asking about your past seems to upset you, Herman. Maybe you'd feel better with a clear conscience. Believe me, I've heard everything. I dated Nunzio, after all. He used to tell me stories that would curl a dead man's toes. Listen, Herman." She reached across and patted his hand. "Your past may have involved a life of crime, but you can always repent. Confession is good for the soul."

The small silence lasted what seemed like an eternity, and the ladies exchanged a look.

Ida opened her mouth to speak, but Nans held her finger to her lips, shushing her.

At last, Herman crumbled. "All right, it's true. I've hated hiding my secrets all these years. I'm an honest man at heart, and I do have a confession."

A collective gasp issued from Lexy and the ladies.

"I knew it," Ruth said over the phone line. "Tell me how you did it, Herman. Did you know Sherman Wilson would be at my storage bay, or was it a coincidence that the two of you arrived there at the same time to search for Nunzio's list in my car?"

"Huh?" Herman said, sounding genuinely perplexed. "Nunzio's list? What're you talking about?"

"Oh, come on now, Herman. Everyone knows about the blackmail list Nunzio kept. You didn't want anyone to know you were on it, so you killed Sherman Wilson to protect your secret. That's why you did it, right?"

"I didn't do anything, and I certainly never killed anyone." Through the plant leaves, Lexy saw Herman toss his napkin angrily onto the table, his voice suddenly as sober as a funeral. "Nor would I ever blackmail anyone. That's not what I was going to confess, Ruth. I've never heard of this list you're talking about either." He leaned closer to Ruth and whispered, "What I was going to tell you about was the bank heist Nunzio and I pulled off fifty years ago."

Before Lexy knew what was happening, Nans was out of her seat and heading around the potted plants to make a beeline for Ruth's table. Lexy and the ladies followed behind her.

"Bank robbery?" Nans said as she approached their table. "You mean you didn't kill Sherman Wilson?"

Several nearby patrons turned to stare, and Lexy moved in beside her grandmother. "You might want to keep your voice down, Nans."

"Oh, posh," Nans scoffed. "These people should mind their own business anyway. Answer my question, Herman Conti."

"Um, no." Herman seemed taken aback by the elderly female inquisition that had now surrounded his and Ruth's table. "I wasn't even in town when Wilson was killed. I swear."

"You all might as well pull up chairs," Ruth said, scooting over. "No sense having the whole town overhear us. We're already splashed across the World Wide Web."

The ladies each took a seat, then Herman continued.

"Look, you're right, Ruth. Nunzio and I weren't always enemies. We actually grew up together as kids in Cold Springs. That's how we knew each other. But I didn't really associate with him much until we were both in our twenties. I'd been a demolitions expert in the army and had just gotten out. Nunzio needed money, as usual." Herman snorted then shook his head, lost in memories. "I remember him coming to me that day, saying he had this scheme to rob the local bank and he needed some explosives for his heist. Normally, I would've told him to get lost, but unfortunately, I needed funds too, so I took the job."

He sighed and rubbed the bridge of his nose. "Listen, I'm not proud of what I did, but I didn't actually *break* into the bank. All I did was supply Nunzio with the charges he needed to blow off the safe door. And the way he explained it, it wasn't even like we were stealing from an innocent person. Nunzio swore the only safety deposit box he targeted belonged to a crime boss. So, really, we were like Robin Hood. Robbing from the bad guy to give to the poor—us."

"What exactly did Nunzio take from the safety deposit box?" Helen asked. "I couldn't find any record of what was stolen on the Internet. Seems no one ever reported the missing items."

"Well, it isn't like a crime boss can file a claim for his stolen goods that were already stolen to begin with," Herman said, chuckling. "The bank did report the break-in and the damage to their safe, for insurance purposes, but everything else was all quickly swept under the rug. I'm guessing someone paid off the cops at the time."

Ida narrowed her gaze on him. "How does this all tie into Sherman Wilson's murder?"

"Not sure," Herman said. "Maybe it was one of the other guys who helped Nunzio break into the safety deposit box. I never knew who they were."

"That would make sense," Lexy said. "And Jack told me Sherman had been in jail for a bank robbery. Maybe he was in on the original heist."

"If that's the case, though, why would he risk getting caught skulking around Ruth's car and possibly returning to prison at his age?" Nans asked.

"Like I said, I wasn't at the robbery itself, so I have no actual proof of what was in that safety deposit box," Herman said. "But, from what I was told way back when, the box was filled with all kinds of treasure—diamonds, gold, lots of rare coins worth millions. At the time, I remember Nunzio fenced the jewels and gold right away, to get the money quickly, but he hid the coins away for later, fearing someone might recognize them if they hit the market too soon. Every once in a while, rumors about the crime and the hidden stash of rare coins make their way around the underworld. The incident is now quite infamous in certain circles." Herman shook his head. "Rather like that whole D. B. Cooper mystery. No one ever found the money."

The ladies all exchanged a look. And Lexy couldn't help wondering if maybe that was where all those old coins hidden in Ruth's car had come from.

"And no one ever found this stash?" Ida asked.

"Nope." Herman pulled out his wallet and handed two twenties and the check to their waitress as she passed by the table. "A few of the coins have surfaced over the years, but never the really rare ones. Lately, though, I've heard a couple new rumors that those coins have made an appearance here in Brooks Ridge Falls."

"Nunzio was an antiques dealer, so he had ties with all sorts of sources." Ruth frowned. "Plus, I remember him belonging to a bunch of forums online. They used to talk for hours and hours about those rare coins."

Herman took his change from the server then sipped his water. "Word on the street and in the forums is that the coins from that heist are finally reentering circulation. The search is still on for the most valuable one of the bunch, though. That one has yet to be found—a 1913 Liberty Head V nickel worth about four million dollars."

"Four million dollars?" Nans sat back, her expression astonished. "For a nickel? Who knew a hunk of metal could be so valuable?"

"I still don't see what this has to do with my condo,"

Ruth said. "Why would they search my place? And how would a thief trace those coins to my car? I'm the only one who knew about all that old change in that Olds."

"Perhaps not the only one, my darling. See, that's where Nunzio's forums come in," Herman said, smiling. "I still keep tabs on those from time to time. Recently, I spotted a post from someone claiming to be an old prison-mate of Nunzio's associates from the heist. This person stated this prison-mate had leaked the location of that rare coin and said it was stashed inside an old car that had belonged to Nunzio just prior to his death."

"Oh my," Ruth gasped, placing her hand over her heart. "My poor Olds."

"Yes, my darling. That's why I've been so worried about you." Herman reached over and took Ruth's other hand. "Believe me. It wasn't me who killed Sherman Wilson or went looking for that coin. Why would I? I certainly don't need that coin. I've got plenty of money on my own. Besides, some things are more important than wealth."

Lexy melted a bit at the sweetness of Herman's statement. It was obvious he was smitten with Ruth. She sighed. She and Jack had been in love with each other like that too, once upon a time. For her, that love was stronger than ever. For Jack? That remained to be seen in Lexy's mind. First she'd have to deal with that mysterious blonde, then she and her husband needed to have a long heart-to-heart talk about their relationship and their future...

"So it seems we've been barking up the wrong tree," Helen said. "Looks like this Sherman Wilson's murder has nothing to do with Nunzio's list and everything to do with a rare coin."

"Yes," Nans said. "Now all we need to do is figure out who else knew about this coin, and we'll have our killer."

# CHAPTER FIFTEEN

"To heck with finding the killer," Ida said as they rushed back into Ruth's apartment a short time later. The layout was the same as Nans' condo, but in reverse. Next to the lavishness of Herman's house before, Ruth's current abode looked downright austere— beige furniture, beige walls, beige carpet and tile. A few framed photos were scattered around the place, mainly of Ruth and her late husband, George, together and one or two of Ruth and Nunzio.

But even though the furnishings were plain, the place smelled divine. Ruth had vases overflowing with lilacs, and the air was happy with the fresh floral scent. There was a tall etched crystal vase on the table, dripping with lavender blossoms, a bulbous squatty round vase on the kitchen counter, stuffed with trailing white flowers, and there were smaller vases lining the pass-through counter, each with dark-purple blooms sprouting from the top.

"I want to find that four-million-dollar coin Herman told us about," Ida said, making a beeline for the round oak table in the center of the dining room area. "Where are they?"

"Let's not forget that Herman knew about the coins. He admitted it in the restaurant," Nans cautioned. "I don't see why we let him go. He could be the killer."

"Herman?" Helen scrunched up her nose. "He's too nice. Besides, he has an alibi. He wasn't in town."

"So he says," Nans said. "We should check that first before ruling him out."

"We will," Helen said.

"Looks like they cleaned up from the break-in quickly," Lexy said while Ruth fixed them a tray of tea and cookies in the pass-through kitchen.

"Yes, thankfully. To think someone would toss my place to try and find that stupid coin."

Ruth shuddered. "Whoever it was, they gave me quite a fright. They're just lucky Nunzio wasn't around. He would've dealt with them fast, and not very nicely, either."

"Coins?" Ida said again, snapping her fingers, her tone impatient.

Nans gave her friend a look. "Let me see if I can find

them." She reached into her large patent-leather handbag and pulled out a small mason jar filled with the coins they'd pulled from the Olds. She unscrewed the lid and spilled them out onto the table then spread them out into one layer. "Let's go through these one by one while Helen looks them up on her iPad."

"Got you covered," Helen said, pulling out her tablet and firing it up. "Ready."

Ruth brought out the refreshments, and Lexy helped her set them out, then they all got to searching. Twenty minutes later, however, they'd still not found the four-million-dollar winner, just a few silver dimes and a couple of old quarters that were worth about a dollar each.

"So much for anything valuable," Ruth said, sighing.

"Oh no!" Ida said, her expression aghast. "You don't think it was one of the ones we used in the slot machines last month, do you?"

"Don't be ridiculous," Ruth said, frowning. "Those casinos don't take real coins anymore, remember? You have to feed your bills in, and then they give you that ticket thing at the end of your games. I distinctly remember because you got into a heated discussion with that nice older fellow who was running the cashier cage because you wanted a free bucket for your coins, and when he tried to explain that you wouldn't need one, you told him exactly where he could get off and how to get there. Why, Lexy, I'm telling you, I've never been so mortified in all my—"

Ida jutted her chin out, a sure sign of trouble. "For your information, those new slot machines are ridiculous. And I was nothing but nice to that cashier until he started to treat me like a helpless little old lady. Heck, I could bench press him and that slot machine receipt maker contraption with one hand tied behind my back. Why, I should've done more than tell him off. I should've—"

"Wait a minute!" Nans frowned over at Ruth and Ida, cutting off their less-than-titillating discussion about modern slot machine protocol. "What about that jewelry you had made, Ruth? The earrings and bracelet. Those were coins from your car, right?"

"Yes, they were." Ruth hurried into the other room and returned with the box Joe had given her the other day. She also brought a necklace Lexy hadn't seen before and laid it on the table. "Let's see if any of these match, Helen."

Helen leaned closer and snapped a few photos then downloaded them into the search engine she was using. "Nope. No match."

"Shoot." Ida sat back and crossed her arms. "What

about your new charm bracelet? Joe made that for you too, right?"

Ruth clasped her wrist reflexively. "Oh, I don't have it right now. It's at the jewelers. I'm getting the clasp fixed from when I caught it on the bumper the other day. It's after five now, and they're closed. I can't call them until tomorrow."

Lexy exhaled. Seemed they were at a dead end yet again. Then she remembered something Jack had mentioned the other night. "The police found a coin at the storage bay during their investigation. Jack said it was close to the front bumper, so I assumed it must've come from Ruth's bracelet when the clasp broke. Remember how I mentioned that to you, Ruth?"

The ladies turned to look at Lexy in unison.

"That's perfect, dear," Nans said. "Think you can sweet-talk that husband of yours into letting us in to take a look at it?"

Lexy's stomach cramped. Given the current precarious situation between her and Jack, she wasn't sure she could get him to tell her the time, let alone let her and the ladies sneak into the evidence room. She didn't want to say that aloud, though. Nans and her friends would only worry, and the last thing Lexy wanted right now was them fussing over her and making her feel worse about what may or may not be happening between Jack and that mysterious blonde. She cleared her throat and forced a smile. "Let me talk to him tonight, and I'll tell you all first thing in the morning."

"Fine, dear." Nans smiled. "Jack's such a nice man."

Lexy didn't answer, just pushed to her feet, making a show of checking her watch. "Look at the time. I really should get home. Jack will be wondering where I am."

She said a hasty goodbye, promising to call Nans tomorrow, then headed out, hoping to beat her husband home to give herself time to prepare.

CHAPTER SIXTEEN

hankfully, Jack's car wasn't in the driveway when Lexy pulled in fifteen minutes later. Good. She needed to get her thoughts centered, get her emotions under control, so she could confront him calmly and rationally about what she'd seen in his office between him and the blonde. She didn't want to be distrustful or suspicious. It went against her nature. But the mounting evidence that he was hiding something from her was growing too strong to ignore.

First his odd behavior the night he'd brought her wine and flowers, when he never brought her wine and flowers. Then the weird conversation she'd overheard between Cassie and John, about not telling her whatever it was Jack was trying to hide. Then the blonde. Nope. Something was definitely going on, and she intended to get to the bottom of it, sooner rather than later. First, though, she needed a bit of time alone. Alone in the Baker-Perillo household, however, was relative, considering Sprinkles waited gleefully at the front door with her usual exuberant greeting.

"Hey, girl," Lexy said, bending to pet the tiny dog and lavish her with attention. At least there was one being in her life who loved her unconditionally. She picked her up and cradled her against her chest, chuckling as Sprinkles kissed her cheek then snuggled her cold, wet nose into Lexy's ponytail. "How's my baby tonight, huh? Were you a good girl today?"

Sprinkles squirmed in doggy ecstasy in Lexy's arms, and Lexy set her down then toed off her shoes and headed into the kitchen. "Are you hungry, huh?" she asked Sprinkles. "Want Mommy to get you some dinner?"

Sprinkles yipped then sat near her bowls.

"All right then." Lexy laughed and pulled a covered can of dog food from the fridge. "Let me get that for you."

As she fixed the dog's dinner, the sound of an engine rumbled in the driveway. Jack was home. *Crap.* Her pulse kicked a notch higher as she set Sprinkles' food dish on the floor for her then ran around the kitchen, messing things up a bit to make it look as if she'd been home for a while. She pulled out a plate of leftovers from the night before and the rest of the bottle of wine Jack had brought home the other day. She poured a generous portion of the chardonnay down the drain before placing a splash in a glass she pulled from the cupboard. The leftovers, unfortunately, went into the trash, and the dirty plate into the sink. Her stomach rumbled, but there wasn't time to eat anything, as the front door opened and Jack appeared, looking as hand-some and jovial as ever while Lexy felt as if she'd just run a one-minute mile.

She patted her hair and forced a smile, her ponytail mussed from running around, and adding to her couch potato appearance, she hoped.

"Hey, honey." Jack walked over and gave her a quick kiss. "How was your day?"

"Good, fine. Uneventful." She kept her smile wide and leaned her elbow against the counter, trying to look relaxed despite the butterflies rioting inside her. "How was yours?"

What she'd really wanted to ask him was about the blonde in his office, but she refrained. No sense starting an argument so early in the evening. They had hours ahead for that, especially if Jack caught on as to why she wanted to see that stupid coin he had in custody.

"Good," he said, taking her by the hand and pulling her into the living room to sit beside him on the sofa. He toed off his shoes then snuggled her into his side. "Busy but good."

Their relationship had always been built on trust. To have that shaken now left Lexy feeling decidedly unsettled. "That's great." She patted him on the thigh as Sprinkles jumped up to sit between them. "That must be why you're in such a good mood, huh?"

*That or the blonde.*

Lexy forced the traitorous idea from her mind. "Would you like some wine?"

"I'd love some, thanks."

"Be right back." She went to the kitchen and grabbed the bottle and two glasses then returned to the living room to pour them both a serving. "How'd your interrogations go today?"

"Huh?" He gave her a confused look before covering fast. "Oh, fine. I think you'll be happy about the result, actually."

"Really?" Lexy sank back into her seat, handing Jack his glass. "Why would I care about your interrogations?"

"Because I can put to rest the crazy notion Mona and her friends had about that Herman Conti fellow," Jack said.

"Really?" Lexy said, sipping her wine then watching Jack over the rim. Had Jack discovered Herman was out of town as he'd said? That would be convenient and one less thing for Lexy and the ladies to do.

"Yeah, he was out of town. Couldn't have done it."

"Well, I'm glad. That Herman Conti always seemed like such a nice old gentleman when he came into my bakery." She leaned over to set her glass on the table then decided to work her way around to the coin issue. "Nans did have a new idea that the murder might have something to do with an old bank heist."

She watched her husband's reaction closely, hoping to get him talking about the coin again, but no luck.

Jack shrugged and took a big gulp of wine. "No kidding."

Stunned, Lexy narrowed her gaze. "You know about the bank heist?"

"Sure, honey. I told you a while ago that the victim was a bank robber, and I am a police officer. I have my sources."

Fine. He wanted to play coy? Then she was done beating around the bush. "You know about the coins then."

"Yeah." He stretched out his legs. "We got a tip about old coins resurfacing in town." Jack glanced at her. "My question is, what do *you* know about it?"

"Only what I told you," Lexy said, giving him her best

LEIGHANN DOBBS

innocent look. Turnabout was fair play these days. If he wanted to keep his secrets, she'd keep hers. For now.

"Hmm," he said, sitting back and not sounding entirely convinced. "I hope that's true, honey. These stolen coins are worth big bucks, and things could get very dangerous. And I don't want you sniffing around Stan at the storage lot either, okay? If anything happened to you and you got hurt, I don't know what I'd do."

*Get comfort from the blonde?*

Lexy frowned, doing her best to silence her inner critic. Snarky thoughts wouldn't help her right now. She needed to stay cool, calm, collected. And focus on the case. Why was Jack worried about Stan, anyway? "Has something come up about Stan?"

Jack rubbed his eyes then laid his head back against the sofa cushions. "He's already lied about his alibi. Who knows what else he could be lying about. Just let us do our jobs, all right?"

"Of course."

Jack looked as tired as she felt, and despite all the problems and things they needed to discuss, all Lexy seemed to want to do at that moment was cuddle up to her husband and forget about everything for a while. She sighed and snuggled into his side, loving the warm weight of his arm around her shoulders. Still, her inquisitive mind wouldn't let the Stan matter drop without one

148

last question. "So Stan the storage man isn't being forthcoming with the truth, eh?"

Jack gave her a look, brow raised, and Lexy quickly turned her face into his chest, kissing his neck above the starched white collar of his shirt to cover her over-eagerness. "Not that I'm planning to go back there at all. Bad memories."

"Uh-huh." Jack chuckled. "That's good because Stan's up to some shenanigans, and it would be best if you and the ladies stayed clear. Until we get things handled."

His phone buzzed, and Jack pulled it out, scowling down at the screen. "Sorry, honey. I need to take this."

He dropped a quick kiss on the top of her head then stood and walked into the kitchen to answer the call. Lexy missed the heat of him immediately but forced herself to remain in her seat. Jack usually never let his work invade his personal life, even going so far as to shut off his phone at night when he was home unless he was on call at the station.

He wasn't on call tonight.

Lexy scooted into the corner of the couch and drew her legs beneath her, stroking her fingers through Sprinkles' soft fur. Suspicions swirled inside her head, making her anxious. She'd let her emotions get the better of her and had cuddled instead of having the hard conversation she knew they needed to have tonight. If he did have something going on with the blonde, it was best to confront it head on—no matter how difficult—and work to resolve the issue.

But Jack was home now and acting normal. He was the same old Jack, and she knew that he couldn't just come home and act normal if he had another woman. That just wasn't the Jack she knew. But if he didn't have something going on with the blonde, then what in the world *was* going on with him?

Low murmurs issued from the kitchen as Jack spoke to his caller, but she was too far away to decipher exactly what he was saying. She only heard the occasional word or sentence—"looking forward to it," "can't wait," "like it was meant to be." None of them helped ease her concerns. Stewing in her love and anxiety for Jack was getting her nowhere.

Lexy held Sprinkles closer and focused on what she'd just learned from Jack instead.

Stan the storage man had lied about his alibi, but why? Did he have something to hide too? Seemed secrets were the order of the day all around. The guy knew about Ruth's car and had access to her storage unit too. Perhaps he even had access to tools like the titanium drill bits, given that all his storage units were metal.

*Stan's up to some shenanigans...*

Shenanigans of the lethal variety? Had he been Sherman Wilson's killer?

She filed all that information away for the morning. Maybe she and the ladies would have to look at Stan a bit more closely. Lexy clicked on the TV instead, hoping to distract herself with the nightly news.

# CHAPTER SEVENTEEN

The next morning, Lexy couldn't wait to get over to Nans' and tell the ladies what she'd discovered from Jack. As luck would have it, there was a mad rush at the bakery, so she spent the morning ringing up sales of Danishes, brownies, whoopie pies, cookies, and bars. The new wave-shaped butter cookies with blue icing waves went like hotcakes, and Lexy made a mental note to double the batch next time.

When the throng of customers dwindled to a slow trickle, she hung up her apron—a vintage pattern of cartoonish vegetables with smiling faces—threw a dozen pastries in a box, and left Cassie in charge while she drove her sputtering VW over to the Brook Ridge Retirement Center.

Ida answered the door, her eyes seeking out the familiar white pastry box. It was getting so that when

Lexy came over, Ida's gaze immediately went to Lexy's hand in search of the box instead of Lexy's face to greet her.

Ida took the box and shoved Lexy inside, where Ruth, Helen, and Nans were congregated around the dining room table, going over the Wilson murder case.

"Hi, dear. I put the dessert plates out on the kitchen counter," Nans said without looking up from the iPad screen she and Helen had their heads bent over.

Lexy took the box back from Ida, who had already pulled out a scone, and went to the kitchen, piling the assortment of éclairs, scones, and doughnuts onto the etched green depression glass platter, then taking five matching doily-lined green dessert plates out to the table. She set the pastries down, and the ladies dug in as she relayed the information she'd learned from Jack the previous night.

"So Herman might've been telling the truth?" Ruth straightened in her seat, the look on her face telling Lexy that maybe Ruth's insistence that she had no romantic inclinations toward Herman was all a bunch of hot air.

"According to Jack, he couldn't have been the killer. His alibi checks out. I don't know if he was telling the truth about all the other stuff, but he does seem very nice." Lexy broke off a piece of scone and put it in her mouth. "If he was once in organized crime, it seems like he gave it up long ago."

"And Jack said that Stan seems to have some shady dealings on the side then? Interesting," Helen said, helping herself to a bear claw. "Did you get Jack's permission for us to look at that coin today?"

"No. I didn't get a chance to ask him. Sorry." Lexy picked an éclair up off the tray and put it on her plate. After Jack had taken his phone call, he'd been acting even more distant and distracted than he had before. They'd had a quick dinner, then she'd turned in early for the night. "He got a work call, so I went to bed early."

Sleep had eluded her, though. She'd tossed and turned most of the night and ended up getting up before dawn to go into the bakery early. Jack had been sound asleep when she'd left.

"Well, don't worry, dear," Nans said, patting her hand. "All married couples go through rough patches at one point or another. I'm sure it's nothing to worry about. Your love will get you through."

"So true," Ruth said after devouring half a glazed doughnut in one bite. "Whenever Nunzio and I would have a disagreement, we'd both take a cooling-off period. Even George and I had spats now and again. Why, I remember staying with my mother for nearly a month one time after we'd been married about a year. Marriage isn't for sissies, that's for sure. But even the worst of fights can be overcome if both partners are willing to forgive."

"We didn't fight," Lexy said, staring down at her uneaten pastry. Tears welled in her eyes, though she refused to let them fall. "I almost wish we would. Then maybe that would clear the air between us. I'm just so worried it's much more than a simple misunderstanding this time."

"What exactly are you afraid of, dear?" Nans said, her voice growing concerned. "Jack's always loved you more than anything. Any fool could see that."

Fool was right. Lexy nodded without answering. She'd thought Jack was devoted to her too. The same way she was to him. But maybe she'd been wrong...

"Then let's focus on the case instead," Ida said gently, squeezing Lexy's hand before helping herself to her second strawberry scone. "Maybe that will take your mind off what's happening with Jack."

"Okay." Lexy forced a smile and nibbled on her éclair, not really tasting it. "Sounds good."

"I don't know about Stan being involved in this mess," Nans said. "Even if what Jack says about him is true, it doesn't make any sense that he'd be the killer. Why would he jeopardize his own business like that? If he did want to take out Sherman Wilson, logic says he'd do it at a different location. Not in his own backyard."

"She has a point," Helen agreed. "And how would he have known about the coins in Ruth's car? He may have had access to her storage bay, but those coins were well hidden, out of plain sight."

"Exactly. My intuition is telling me the police are off base here. Not that it matters, though, since they never listen to me." Nans shook her head. "I will say this about that husband of yours, dear. If he has one flaw, it's that Jack's always so intent on following his evidence that he gives no credence to my intuition."

"He'd do well to pay attention to us," Ida said. "We've been right far more than the police over the years."

"True enough," Helen and Ruth agreed.

"Well, it's too late now," Nans said. "We don't have time to change his mind. We need to figure out if Stan really is the murderer before someone else gets killed."

"Yes," Ruth said. "I'd like that. Considering I'm the one at this table who's been targeted."

Ida patted Ruth on the shoulder. "All the more reason we should get to the jewelry store as soon as possible to pick up your bracelet. God forbid that four-million-dollar coin is on there and they ruined it!"

"Will you stop with that coin already?" Helen gave Ida a peeved stare. "If the stupid thing is ruined, then so be it. It couldn't be helped if Ruth had it cut out for her bracelet. Coins are only valuable if they are intact."

"I just wish I had known some of those might be valuable before I had them made into jewelry," Ruth said.

"You'd think Joe would have known," Ida said.

Nans pressed her lips together. "He was arguing with that man about a coin at his place, but he said he knew nothing about coins."

"Well, if that's not true, then he would have switched the coin and we won't find it, anyway." Ida shoved the rest of her scone in her mouth. "Either way, we got ourselves a killer to catch."

"All right then." Ruth set down her cup atop her empty plate. "We should split up to spend our time more wisely."

"Agreed." Nans stood. "Ruth and Helen, you go to the jewelers to get the bracelet. It's only a short walk from here." She turned to Lexy and smiled. "My granddaughter and I and Ida will go talk to Stan."

# CHAPTER EIGHTEEN

*L*exy was growing more concerned about her yellow VW Bug as it groaned and sputtered to a stop outside Stan's office at the storage facility. What if it died completely and left them stranded? This might not be a good place, especially if Stan was mixed up in the murder.

The place currently looked deserted, except for Stan, who stood in the front doorway to his office, hands on hips, looking not at all pleased to see them. His scowl only darkened as Lexy, Nans, and Ida stepped from the vehicle and approached him.

The tightness in Lexy's shoulders increased. As much as she hated to admit it at the moment, given Stan's menacing presence today, it was entirely possible Jack had been right about the guy being dangerous and the ladies needing to stay away from him. He was wearing a stained wifebeater, and his hairy, tattooed arms were crossed firmly over his protruding beer belly, making him look as if he'd walked right off the set of *The Sopranos*.

Considering they were all but standing on his doorstep, however, it was too late to turn back.

"What are you doing here?" Stan demanded, his tone far gruffer than usual, as if he'd just rolled out of bed or smoked an entire carton of cigarettes. "Haven't you people caused enough trouble around here?"

"We haven't even started yet," Nans said, continuing toward Stan, undeterred. Lexy had to hand it to her petite grandmother. Not only was she brave—staring down a guy who stood six inches taller than her and outweighed her by more than half—but she didn't mince words, either. Nans continued walking until she climbed up two steps of the front stoop to stand nose to chest with the guy, drawing herself up to her full five-foot-one height. "Tell us what you know about those coins. Or we'll make you wish you never set foot in Brook Ridge Falls."

Stan raised a brow. "Yeah? You and what army?"

Nans pointed to Lexy. "Her husband is the lead homicide detective working on the Sherman Wilson murder investigation, Stan. You think he hasn't dug up all kinds of dirt on you already? In fact, I know beyond a shadow of a doubt that he's already planning to form a

SWAT team to raid this place as we speak. All he needs is one phone call from my granddaughter to do it. Do you really want to take that chance, Stan?"

Of course, Lexy had said no such thing to Nans or the ladies. This was all her grandmother's way of getting Stan to talk. She didn't say a word, just stared down the guy along with Ida by her side.

At the mention of the SWAT team, Stan visibly blanched. "Uh, I don't want no more trouble around here. Just tell me what you want, and we can all settle this peacefully."

Snorting, Nans poked him in the chest with her index finger. "The coins, Stan. Where are they?"

"Coins? I don't know nothing about any coins. I swear." He took a step back, hands in the air. "Honest. All I do know is you meddling old ladies better skedaddle if you know what's good for you. Whatever you're up to, you don't know who you're dealing with. If you keep playing this game, you're going to get hurt." His stern expression softened a bit as he gazed down at Nans. "And I don't want you to get hurt. You remind me of my grandma."

"I'll show you grandma, mister." Ida shoved in beside Nans, nose scrunched as she stared down Stan. "What game are you talking about? The only game we're playing is whether we call the cops on you now or later, buddy."

"The game of you gals coming here, asking about what cars were on the premises the morning that body was found when you know darn well what cars were here." He frowned down at Ida. "And don't you dare threaten me, granny." He sneered at her. "In fact, now that I think about it, maybe *you all* were the ones involved with this coin business that has the police swarming all over. Maybe you all are trying to frame *me*." His gaze narrowed on Nans and Ida. "How's that for a threat?"

"That's absolute nonsense." Nans took a step back, giving Stan an incredulous look. "We weren't anywhere near this storage facility the night of the murder, and we certainly didn't kill anyone. The police have already cleared us, which is way more than I can say for you."

"Really?" Stan snorted. "Then why did I see your car here that morning? And why are you back here now, getting all nosy into the police's case, huh?"

"You mean that VW Bug?" Ida said, pointing to Lexy's car. "Now we have proof you're lying. That car wasn't anywhere near here the morning we found the body. It was across town in the garage, being repaired."

"No," Stan said, his tone exasperated. "Not that hunk of junk."

"Hey!" Lexy said, giving him a dirty look.

"I'm talking about the silver station wagon that you

all showed up in the other day when Ruth started giving me the third degree. That car was here the morning the body was found." He raised his chin defiantly, crossing his arms once more. "Then again, you already knew that, didn't you? Since you ladies came here in it. Only thing I can't figure out is how you four little old ladies managed to take down a big guy like Wilson. Must've tag teamed him or something."

Ida opened her mouth to let the guy have it again, but Lexy cut her off.

"Silver station wagon?" she said, confused. "I don't own a silver station wagon."

"No." Nans snapped her fingers. "You don't, but Myra does." She gave Stan a steely-eyed stare. "Much as it pains me to admit, he's right. That car was here the morning we found the body, but not until later. That's the vehicle Myra used to pick us up in that day, remember?"

"That wasn't the only time, though," Stan said, shifting his weight and causing his tank top to ride higher, showing off a pale, hairy expanse of his flabby gut. Lexy scrunched her nose and looked away fast. "That station wagon was here earlier too."

"It was?" the ladies said in unison.

"Yep." Stan crossed his arms and gave them a skeptical look. "Don't act like you didn't know. Always trying to pull a fast one on everybody, acting like a bunch of nice old ladies, when in reality you're a pit of vipers. That's what you are."

Ida turned and hissed at Stan, laughing when he flinched. "Beware of the serpent, Stan, or you'll get bit!"

Nans rolled her eyes then glanced over at Lexy, frowning. "Myra said they use that car for their Uber business. Joe drives it too, just depending on which one of them is available when a call comes in."

"And Joe would know all about those coins," Ida added. "That's his business, after all."

"But he told the man he was arguing with that he didn't know about the coins," Lexy said.

Ida gave her an incredulous look. "He lied. Plain and simple. And with good reason. He's been scamming those jewelry customers. And if he really does know coins, he's probably involved in those forums Herman mentioned. He might have heard the rumors about the coins being in Brook Ridge Falls."

"Come on, girls," Nans said, grabbing Lexy by the elbow and dragging her back toward the Bug before she could protest. "Looks like we've got a new suspect on our radar, and I think I know just where we can find him."

"What about Stan?" Ida said, glowering at the storage man over her shoulder. "I could take that guy."

"Listen, no one's taking anyone," Lexy said, unlocking

the car doors then holding the seat for Ida so she could climb into the backseat. "And the only place we're heading now is the police station. If Joe Stoddard is somehow involved, Jack needs to know."

She got behind the wheel and started the engine, praying that she wouldn't run into the blonde in her husband's office again today.

# CHAPTER NINETEEN

*W*hile Lexy drove at top speed over to the police station—which in the Bug these days was about thirty-five—Nans sat in the passenger seat and checked her messages on her phone.

"Darn. Ruth said the jeweler's isn't open. They have a handwritten sign tacked up in the door. Something about a family emergency and that they'd be back shortly." Nans sighed and stared out the window beside her, frowning. "Looks like we'll have to wait to find out if that valuable coin is on her bracelet or not."

Lexy drove the last few blocks to the police station, gripping the steering wheel tight. Not only was she nervous about her poor car making the journey intact, she was worried about what Jack would say when she showed up again unexpectedly. Just a week ago, she never would have had any doubts about popping into this office unannounced. She'd done that a lot since they'd been married, taking him special batches of her treats or just leaning her head into his office to say hi.

Over the last year or so, though, they'd both gotten so busy—him with his police work and her with the bakery —that such fun interludes had grown sparser. Maybe that was why he'd gone looking elsewhere for attention and affection. She winced at the ache in her chest. Perhaps she was as guilty as he was of neglecting their relationship. Guilt now joined the hurt inside her.

She signaled and slowed to turn into the police head-quarters parking lot, a lump of sadness clogging her throat. Was it too late to bare their souls and their secrets and save the love she and Jack had?

The car coasted into a parking spot just as the engine sputtered out a cough, wheezed, and then died. Hope-fully it just needed a rest and would start later. Lexy said a silent prayer of thanks then got out, helping Ida from the backseat. The ladies walked arm in arm up to the station entrance. Considering what they'd just discovered at Stan's about Joe Stoddard's possible involvement in the Sherman Wilson murder, Lexy had no doubt leaving this whole thing in Jack's capable hands was the best solution all around.

Still, she just wished she didn't dread seeing him again so much.

It wasn't that she didn't love spending time with the man she loved. She just didn't relish the doubt crouching between them like gremlins. The truth would win out in the end. Lexy only wished it didn't hurt so bad to wait.

The lobby was empty, and Nans and Ruth's orthopedic shoes squeaked on the industrial tile as they rushed past the receptionist. In the background, they could hear muted sounds of phones ringing, a door buzzing, and the quiet murmur of the dispatcher talking into the headset.

A burst of laughter filtered out of one of the break rooms, and Lexy wondered if it might be Jack and the blonde, but it was only a cluster of uniformed officers with Styrofoam cups in their hands. The station smelled of stale coffee and cleaning chemicals.

As Lexy made her way to Jack's office, she experienced the claustrophobic sensation that a prisoner might feel as he was being led to the jail cells at the back of the building. She shrugged it off and held her breath as she halted in her husband's doorway.

Thankfully, the blonde was nowhere to be seen today. Lexy wasn't exactly sure what she would've done had the other woman been there, but given her skyrocketing stress levels at the moment, it wouldn't have been

LEIGHANN DOBBS

pretty. After a deep breath to steady her shaking hands, she knocked on the wood doorframe. "Hey."

Jack looked up from his paperwork, his expression surprised. "Honey, what are you doing here? What a pleasant surprise!"

"It is?" she asked, hesitant.

"Always." He got up and walked over to kiss her. "I love seeing you almost as much as I love you, period."

Love for him squeezed the air from her lungs. What was wrong with her? She'd let her overactive imagination put a barrier between her and Jack. She'd jumped to conclusions about the blonde and the conversation between John and Cassie. She'd even imagined the worst about his unaccountable awkwardness when he'd brought her wine and flowers. But still, the niggling sensation that *something* was going on persisted. Why couldn't he just tell her what the heck was going on?

"We have another suspect for you," Nans said, pushing into his office past Lexy and jarring her out of her thoughts. "Joe Stoddard."

"Really? Joe Stoddard? Doesn't he run a taxi service in town?"

"What difference does that make?" Ida said, plopping down into one of the chairs in front of Jack's desk. "Uber drivers can be killers too."

Jack sighed and sat back in his chair, his smile fading

into consternation. "Look, ladies, I've indulged you all enough. Probably way more than I should because I love my wife. But let's look at the facts in this case. First, the other day you wanted me to arrest this poor Herman Conti guy, but that turned out to be a false alarm. Now, you expect me to arrest Joe Stoddard and bring him in for questioning on nothing more than your word?" He ran a hand through his thick brown hair and shook his head. "I'm sorry, Mona, but I can't do it. He's not even on my suspect list. And you've given me no proof."

"Stan the storage man said Joe Stoddard's station wagon was in his parking lot around the time of the murder," Lexy said, standing behind Ida's chair to give herself some space between her and Jack. Standing too close to him distracted her, and right now she needed to keep all of her wits.

Jack scrubbed his hand over his face and gave a mirthless chuckle. "Back to investigating again, honey? Didn't we specifically discuss you not going to Stan's storage facility anymore?"

Heat prickled Lexy's cheeks, and she looked away. "Nans was going, and I didn't want her to be there unprotected."

"I see. And it never occurred to you to call me?" The warmth in his honey-brown eyes dissolved into anger. "I'm telling you that guy is far too dangerous for all of you. Not to mention that car of yours is on its last legs, honey. What would've happened if you'd gotten stranded out there?"

"I had my cell phone," Lexy said, her own irritation rising over his imperious tone. She wasn't some child who needed a keeper. She was a grown woman. She'd bet good money he didn't treat the blonde that way. "If we'd needed help, I would've called."

"Really?" Jack sat back. "Take out your phone, please."

Annoyed, she held his gaze as she dug around in her purse to pull out the device. Once she had it in hand, she thrust it toward her husband like a trophy. "See? Right here."

"Check the screen," he said, his arrogant expression only increasing her ire.

Lexy turned the phone, and her shoulders slumped. Out of juice. Okay, fine. Maybe Jack was right this time. It didn't mean he was correct about everything else or that he had to rub her nose in it. "I have a charger in my car."

"And what would you use to power it up? The battery in your VW is as decrepit as the rest of that vehicle." He sighed and pushed to his feet, exhaling slowly as he walked over to take Lexy's shoulders gently. "Look, I'm sorry, honey. I knew because I tried to call you earlier and it said your number was currently unavailable. Pretty sure that gave me a few gray hairs until you showed up here on my doorstep." He pulled her stiff form into a hug. "I just love you and don't want to see you get hurt."

Her breath caught. See? She'd been overreacting to everything. Jack really did love her.

Jack pulled back slightly and smiled down at her, the one that made her knees tingle and her toes curl. Darn him. That was one powerful weapon where he was concerned. Lexy sighed. "I'm sorry about breaking my promise about going to the storage facility too. And I appreciate you trying to protect me, but we need to discover the truth here and..."

Jack slipped his arm around her waist, his hand on the small of her back as he directed her out the door and toward the lobby. Nans and Ida followed behind them. "I hate to cut this short, honey, but I've got a meeting with the commissioner in about five minutes." He gave her one more quick peck then waved to the other ladies before heading back toward the gate. "You'll find out the truth soon. Don't worry. You won't have to worry about it for much longer."

All of Lexy's doubts came crashing back at Jack's strange parting words.

Stunned, Lexy stood at the front entrance, Nans and

Ida by her side, and watched Jack walk back to his office alone.

*You'll find out the truth soon...*

What was he talking about? She wouldn't have to worry about what? His advice? Their marriage? Her heart sank as she walked back outside and headed toward the car, not missing the strange glance Ida and Nans exchanged. Both the ladies were remaining suspiciously silent now, which only served to heighten Lexy's sense of dread.

Could they tell too that something was horribly wrong between her and Jack? Had it been obvious to everyone but her? Or worse, did they *know* about it just like John and Cassie? And was she partly to blame? Perhaps she had taken the investigating too far this time. Jack's only concern seemed to be for her safety, yet each time he asked her not to go somewhere, she did exactly that.

Was that maybe why he'd taken an interest in the blonde? She was sure Jack wouldn't cheat, but maybe his heart was starting to wander against his will. Was she docile and easily manipulated, doing whatever Jack said without question? When they'd been dating, he'd said that Lexy's fire and spirit were two of the things he loved and admired most about her. Now, though, perhaps that had changed. And was her disregard for his wishes driving him right into the arms of another woman? She loved helping Nans and the other ladies with their cases, but not enough to ruin her marriage. If Jack wanted her to back off, that was what Lexy would do. Just as soon as they got this Sherman Wilson murder solved.

She and the ladies were already in far too deep now to back out.

# CHAPTER TWENTY

"We need to get concrete evidence against Joe Stoddard. That will show Jack we're serious this time. I should have expected this from him. Never listens to me. Not about cases, not about how to handle your—"

Ida coughed loudly from the backseat, cutting Nans off.

"Handle my what?" Lexy asked, keeping her eyes on the road ahead for fear the tears stinging the back of her eyes would well over. That meeting with Jack had been another disaster, not because she'd caught him with the blonde again, but because she'd done nothing but fight with him when she should've been asking him the hard, serious questions that might have gotten her the answers she needed.

"Oh, nothing, dear." Nans and Ida exchanged

another look in the rearview mirror that Lexy didn't miss. It felt as if the whole world were in on the joke and she was the only one left standing in the cold. Surprises had never been her favorite, and now that feeling was only solidified. Her grandmother glanced over at Lexy and frowned. "Are you all right, dear? You haven't said much since we left the station, and you look awfully pale. Maybe you should lie down in my condo for a while when we get back to the retirement center. I don't want you getting sick."

"I'm fine." Lexy forced a smile. The last thing she wanted to do right now was sit in a quiet room by herself and stew in her thoughts even more. "I'm just tired, I guess. Lots going on."

"Hmm." Nans' tone said she didn't buy Lexy's excuse for a second, but thankfully, she let the matter drop. "Well, in that case, we should head over to the Stoddards' place ourselves, once we pick up Ruth and Helen. It's still early yet, and maybe we can find something we can show Jack to compel him to arrest Joe."

Lexy nodded and turned down the street where the retirement center was located. No way would she clue her grandmother into how much Jack's last statement had bothered her. They had enough to manage with the case and Joe and—

*BANG!*

The Bug shuddered from the huge backfire, sputtered, then died completely just as Lexy rolled into the retirement home parking lot. Thankfully, she managed to steer the deceased vehicle into an empty parking spot and jam on the parking break to bring them to a final halt.

"Well, that was a lucky break," Ida said from the backseat. "It's wicked hot outside. Would hate to have to walk for any great distance today."

"It was time, honey. I'm sorry." Nans reached over and patted Lexy's hand, which was still poised on the gearshift. "But who knows—maybe something better is waiting right around the corner."

Lexy blinked back tears and reached for her purse. Her first instinct was to call her husband, but she stopped herself. With everything else going on between them, her letting him know that he'd been right about her car and they'd have to replace it soon too could be the last straw. Blinking hard into the sunlight, she rubbed the VW's dashboard lovingly and said a heartfelt, silent goodbye to the best car a girl had ever owned.

"Great," Ida said, throwing up her hands. "How are we supposed to get to the Stoddards' now? The sign on the bank over there says it's close to ninety."

"Let's rest a minute. Maybe the car will start again," Nans said, though her expression said chances were slim.

They rolled down the windows, and a slight breeze blew in, keeping the atmosphere inside the car from becoming stifling. A large shade tree overhead also helped.

They sat for a few minutes, listening to the engine tick as it cooled down and watching a robin hop along in the grass under the tree. It cocked its head, shiny black eyes sparkling. Then hop, hop, hop, and it stabbed its beak into the ground and came up with a juicy, wriggling worm before flying off, its red breast brightening in the sun. If only things could be that easy for Lexy. But here she was, beloved car about to be no more... and maybe her marriage was designated for the same fate.

Ida sighed and sat back. "Well, I suppose the Stoddards' place isn't far from here," Ida said. "I guess if we take it slow, we could easily walk over there and do a bit of surveillance."

"See? Things are improving already." Nans fished around inside her enormous bag then pulled out her phone again. "If we skulk around the windows, I might be able to snap a few photos of him with an old coin or something. You know, for evidence."

"Jack was right, though. This whole situation is dangerous." Lexy unsnapped her seatbelt. "We need to be careful to avoid detection. If they catch us, we could get in big trouble."

"I'll text Ruth and Helen and have them meet us."

Nans fumbled with her phone, holding it at arm's length and using her thumbs awkwardly.

*Ding!*

"They're coming right down. Ruth says the bracelet didn't have the valuable coin in it." Nans shrugged. "Good thing. It would have been ruined anyway."

"Yeah, that might mean it's still around somewhere. I could use four million," Ida said.

"Who couldn't?" Nans asked.

They lapsed into silence. Lexy imagined Nans and Ida were dreaming about what they would do with four million. She, on the other hand, spent the time worrying about her car and Jack. Ruth and Helen showed up a few minutes later, and they made their way across the parking lot, past the first large condo building, and over to the Stoddards' detached condo.

Whoever had lived in the Stoddards' detached condo before had planted extra shrubs around the property. There was a row of thick azaleas that reached to Lexy's shoulder, some tightly compacted evergreen shrubs, and a row of lush rhododendrons with large, shiny leaves and a few purple petals still clinging to branches. A dusting of spent flowers lay below the bushes. A chipmunk scurried out as they approached.

Lexy and the ladies hunkered down in the shrubbery surrounding the Stoddard home. Even though the dense plants afforded some shade, sweat prickled the back of Lexy's neck, and she adjusted her ponytail to allow the breeze to cool her skin.

"It's hotter than Hades out here," Ruth complained, fanning herself with a leaflet from the Burger Barn she'd found in her purse. "Watch out for snakes in these bushes."

"Ack!" Helen practically jumped into Nans' arms, her eyes wildly searching the ground for a snake.

"She didn't say there *was* a snake, Helen," Nans said. "Just watch for them. They like the heat, so they would probably be over there in the sun."

"Oh, right," Helen adjusted her pink flowered shirt and worked on regaining her composure, her eyes still straying to the ground every few seconds.

"Hey, I think I hear the ice cream truck coming," Ida said, cupping her ear and leaning toward the street. "Boy, I could sure go for a snow cone right about now. Oh shoot!"

"What's wrong?" Ruth asked, concerned. "And keep your voice down. We're undercover."

Ida scowled at her lower leg. "These stupid branches caused a run in my No nonsense pantyhose. Brand new pair too, darn it."

"For goodness' sake, Ida. Be quiet!" Nans scolded her friend. She went to move her big purse and snagged the expensive patent leather on a gnarled branch, getting into a heated tug-of-war with the misbehaving shrub. "I swear if this plant doesn't unhand my belongings, I will get an axe and chop it down."

"Here." Lexy helped her grandmother get the enormous purse untangled then gestured for the ladies to follow her closer to the condo. From there, it was an easy move to scooch up and peek through the nearest window. Lexy peered inside and spotted what looked like a workroom. Against one wall were machines and tools that Lexy guessed would be used in a jewelry-making business—saws, files, hammers, metal dabs, stamps, and punches.

"Look!" Nans gasped, her tone excited. "See that drill over there on the worktable? It looks a lot like the one they found at the crime scene near Sherman Wilson's body."

"And beside it, on the table." Ida crowded in shoulder to shoulder with Lexy. "Gloves. White cotton gloves. Didn't Jack tell you the techs found white fibers on the door lock?"

"Yes, he did," Lexy whispered. "Nans, can you take a few pictures while we're here?"

"Already on it." Nans held up her phone and snapped away through the window.

"Excuse me. What are you doing out here?" a voice

said behind them, making all the ladies jump. Lexy whirled around fast, her pulse stumbling.

There stood Myra Stoddard, staring at them angrily.

Nans fumbled her phone and barely avoided dropping it on the pavement. "Oh, hello, Myra."

"We were just out for a walk," Ida said.

"A walk?" Myra frowned. "In the shrubs behind my house?"

"Actually, we were coming to see you," Lexy said, hoping her lie sounded more convincing because it was partially the truth, even though she was grasping at straws. "Uh, my car just broke down again, and we were hoping you might be able to give us a ride. I would've called, but my phone's dead."

Myra stared at them for a moment, and Lexy wondered if she should repeat what she'd said but louder. Myra tapped the toe of her sparkly sandal against the hot pavement, and her gaze narrowed as if she were deciding whether to give them a ride or call the cops on them for lurking in the bushes. "Okay, fine. I'm free at the moment. Where would you like me to drive you?"

# CHAPTER TWENTY-ONE

Myra's silver station wagon had heated up in the sun, so they left the doors open to let the hot air out. Along with it came the smell of Naugahyde and French fries.

"Sorry, my last ride wanted me to go through the drive-through." Myra bent into the car and pulled out a thin red cardboard French fry holder then shoved it into a trash bag she kept in the front. She hopped in and started the engine. "We'll let the air conditioning run for a few minutes."

Lexy leaned against the car, the heat of the metal burning through her shorts. She glanced back at the Stoddards' condo. She didn't want to leave. She wanted to get more evidence on Joe, but she wasn't sure how to handle Myra. If they told her, she might not believe them and might go to Joe. She could be in danger.

Not to mention that snapping pictures through the windows wasn't going to fly with her standing there watching them. It was probably best that they take the evidence of the drill and the gloves back to Jack. But with her car dead and her cellphone dead, the only way to do that was Myra.

Lexy jumped into the passenger seat, and Nans, Ida, Ruth, and Helen all climbed into the backseat, giving Lexy looks in the rearview mirror as Myra sat behind the wheel.

"You know," Ida started, "the real reason we were lurking behind your building is because—Ow!"

Nans elbowed Ida in the side then shot Lexy a warning look in the rearview mirror. *Keep your mouth shut about Joe,* it screamed as effectively as if her grandmother had shouted the words aloud. Right, it wouldn't be smart to say anything. Myra was his wife and probably wouldn't believe them. Worse, she might warn Joe and blow the whole case. Lexy gave a short nod then clicked her seatbelt into place.

"Where am I taking you?" Myra asked.

"Oh, the police station on Cross Street," Lexy said, giving her a polite smile.

Myra looked wary. "The police? Is there something going on I should know about?"

Lexy opened her mouth to answer, only to be jarred

by a rough kick to the back of her seat, courtesy of Nans. She gave her grandmother a quick glance in the rearview mirror then continued. "Uh, no. No trouble. My husband works there, and he'll give me a ride to get my car fixed."

"Right." Myra stared at Lexy a second longer than normal before shifting the giant silver station wagon into drive. "Your husband's a police officer. Great. Okay then. Let's go."

As they drove through the sun-dappled streets of Brook Ridge Falls, Lexy and the ladies did their best to keep the small talk flowing and Myra distracted from asking any more questions.

"Lovely weather we're having," Helen said, patting her hairspray-lacquered coiffure. Neither heat nor wind nor any mighty gust would disturb that helmet hair.

"Yeah. Drives my allergies nuts, though," Ida chimed in. "Remind me to take another pill when we get back to the retirement center."

"Will do." Nans leaned forward to tap Lexy on the shoulder. "Do you have a tissue, dear?"

"Oh, let me look." As Lexy rifled through her purse, she couldn't help stealing glances at Myra through her lashes. The woman had remained oddly quiet since Lexy had mentioned Jack was a police officer. Fine lines of tension now marked the corners of her mouth too.

Did Myra know about her husband's illegal activity?

A twinge of pity shot through her. If so, then that sort of put them in the same boat, didn't it? Little did poor Myra know, she was driving them to have Joe arrested. At least, that was Lexy's plan, anyway. Between Nans' pictures of the drill and the white gloves, that should be enough to at least bring the man in for questioning, anyway. Still, the connection she now felt for Myra given both of their husbands' hidden secrets had her wanting to know more about their marriage. She pulled a tissue out of the plastic pack in her purse and handed it to Nans then turned to Myra once more. "How long has Joe worked with rare coins?"

Several gasps issued from the back, followed by another hard kick to the back of her seat. Lexy gripped the dashboard tight and frowned at her grandmother in the rearview mirror.

Myra shrugged, seemingly oblivious to the undercurrent of tension in the air. "Not that long, really. A couple of years at the most. Once he retired, it took him a while to settle on a hobby he liked. Good timing too, considering he was about to drive me nuts with all his sitting around and moping." Myra snorted. "Heck, some days I almost wished he'd have an affair or something, just to get him out of the house."

Lexy's grip on the strap of her purse tightened. She and Jack sometimes got on each other's nerves, but she'd never, ever wished for him to stray. Her frown deepened. "Has Joe ever come across any cool coins while making his jewelry?"

They slowed for a red light, and Myra turned to give Lexy an odd look. "What exactly do you mean by cool?"

"Oh, nothing." Lexy did her best to pretend the question was entirely casual. Not exactly easy to do, given all four ladies in the backseat were now leaning forward to peer at them around the head rests as if hanging on Myra's every word. "I didn't mean anything specific, since I know so little about coins." She gave a small chuckle. "I've just heard that some can be quite rare or valuable. At least from what I've read."

The light turned green, but Myra didn't move, her placid expression turning hard and cold. "You heard that argument in front of our condo the other day, didn't you?"

It wasn't really a question.

Heat prickled Lexy's cheeks as Myra's gaze narrowed. Was she asking out of embarrassment or something else entirely? Lexy took a deep breath and tried to explain herself without giving away too much. "We were just walking down the street and saw Joe with that other man. Their voices were a bit loud, so unfortunately, we couldn't really help overhearing. Sorry. But don't worry. I know how disagreeable customers can be sometimes." Honestly, she didn't. Her customers had never been anything but sweet and kind. In fact, if anyone had been that angry about their purchase, Lexy would have been mortified. Still, she'd started this ruse, and now she needed to run with it. She cleared her throat before continuing. "Believe me, with running the bakery, I see people get nasty with each other all the time. They accuse each other of all kinds of awful things..."

A horn honked behind them, and Myra reluctantly turned forward again, her movements more deliberate now as they made a right turn onto Elm Street.

Lexy frowned. "Um, I think you've gotten your locations mixed up, Myra. The police station is on Cross Street. You should've taken Maple, not Elm."

"Oh, it is?" Myra said, her tone sticky sweet. She put on her signal again and made another sharp right, sending the ladies in the backseat tumbling to one side. "I must have misheard you. I guess I'll just go around the block then and head back the way we came from."

"Um, dear?" Nans tapped on Lexy's arm again, distracting her. "You might want to look at Ruth's wrist."

Lexy did so. Ruth was wearing the charm bracelet she'd gotten from the jeweler earlier that day. Big deal. She'd already said the valuable coin wasn't on there, so why was Nans calling attention to...?

Oh wait! The bracelet had all the coins—none missing. Which meant the coin the police had found wasn't from Ruth's bracelet. Her heart skipped a beat. So if the coin near the murder victim hadn't been from Ruth, then...

"What's going on back there?" Myra asked, swerving to miss a squirrel darting across the road. The tires squealed, and Lexy's eyes widened. They were going way too fast for this residential street, and the jarring moves caused the entire vehicle to shudder and sway from side to side. The ladies in the back took the brunt of it, with Myra and Lexy secured in place with the seat belts. Still, stuff was jangling and rustling about, including all of Myra's jewelry—dangly earrings and a flashy copper-colored charm bracelet.

"Weird how Ruth's bracelet isn't missing a charm, huh?" Ida mused from the backseat, as if reading Lexy's thoughts. "Ow! Why'd you—"

"Shhh!" Nans said, her tone stern. "Just hang on and try not to squish me any more than you already have."

Soon, Myra zoomed out of Brook Ridge Falls proper and jerked hard to the left, tearing down a deserted dirt road. The sudden movement caused the visor above Lexy's head to dip precariously, and a paper fluttered out to land in her lap.

"Pardon me for saying so, Myra, but maybe you should slow down a bit," Helen said loudly from the backseat.

Myra didn't answer, just kept barreling down the dirt road at top speed.

Lexy's stomach nosedived to her toes and she glanced at the paper. It was a hospital bill for Joe. According to the document, he'd had hernia surgery the week prior and had just been released Monday night. Even if he was the fastest healer in the world, today was only Thursday. Sherman Wilson had been killed early Tuesday morning. No way could he have murdered that man in such a violent and bloody fashion without significant injury to himself.

Which meant it had to have been another person, someone else who had access to those coins and the tools Joe used to make his jewelry...

Her gaze flew to Myra's wrist again, where her charm bracelet still jangled merrily against the steering wheel.

A charm bracelet made of coins, just like Ruth's.

A charm bracelet with an empty slot where a missing charm should go.

Nans leaned in again, her gaze darting from Lexy to Myra's wrist then back again as they pulled into a secluded area of woods, so far off the beaten path it was unlikely any one would find them—until it was too late. Myra cut the engine, and quiet descended upon them as Nans whispered in Lexy's ear, "Maybe getting a ride wasn't such a good idea after all, eh?"

# CHAPTER TWENTY-TWO

*B*efore any of the ladies could get out of the station wagon, Myra had pulled a gun from her expensive Coach purse and aimed it directly at Lexy. "I saw all of you looking in our windows. I know what you're up to, you know." Her hands shook slightly as she spoke, the glint in her eyes wild. "I should've expected as much from a bunch of nosy old ladies, always meddling in everyone else's business. You might call yourselves the Ladies Detective Club, but all of you ought to have kept your big noses out of our business." She kept the weapon trained on the center of Lexy's chest while giving a quick look back at Nans. "You might be clever, but those wits won't help you now. That's what you get for snooping in my windows."

"We were not snooping," Nans said. "We were just bird watching."

"Did you say bird watching?" Myra scrunched up her face as if she hadn't heard correctly.

Nans nodded.

"The only birds around those shrubs are sparrows. You were looking through our windows, weren't you? Trying to catch my husband doing something wrong."

"Whyever would we do that?" Nans asked.

Myra waved the gun at them. "You're all liars. And not to be trusted. I've got my eyes on you, so keep your hands out of your purses. There's no telling what you people keep in those. No funny business. I want to see you all facing forward and looking me in the eye."

Lexy did her best to remain calm, as Jack had always taught her. His voice rang through her head now—*stay calm, stay focused, remember details to tell the police later.* The irony of the situation wasn't lost on her either. Lesson learned. Be careful what you search for, or you just might find it. Just look what happened to her when she went looking for answers regarding what Jack was hiding. A blonde, to be precise. Now, with a gun pointed at her heart, ready to fire any minute, she'd never get the chance to ask him point-blank for the truth.

Lexy took a deep breath and closed her eyes, a faint clicking noise like the tapping of keys echoing in her head. She squinted one eye open to see Ida, head up, eyes forward on Myra, a suspiciously innocent look plastered on her face. From where Myra sat facing them, right in front of Ida, she wasn't privy to what Lexy could see from her angle in the passenger seat. Ida's hands were hidden behind her gigantic purse, her fingers furiously typing in a text on Nans' phone.

She glanced at Myra, who didn't appear the least bit suspicious. Her hearing problems prevented her from hearing the faint clicking sound!

Lexy's hope sprouted wings. Perhaps help would reach them in time after all.

Myra snorted. "You all think you're so smart, don't you? Think you're such great sleuths, but look how easily I got you into my car. There wasn't even a struggle. You all just jumped right in. And if kidnapping you was such a piece of cake, shooting you will be like shooting fish in a barrel." She waved the barrel of the gun closer to Lexy's face. "Out of the car. Now. And don't even think about trying anything. That goes for any of you. I've been known to have a twitchy trigger finger, and I'm not afraid to fire."

They all got out of the vehicle, and Myra herded them into a small group on the passenger side of the station wagon. "Great. Now start walking toward that cliff."

"But that leads down to the river," Ruth said. "I can't swim."

"Swimming is the least of your worries now." Myra smiled, cold and sinister. "Don't worry. You'll be dead long before you hit the water. Today, there's going to be a tragic accident within the local geriatric community."

Slowly, the ladies backed away toward the cliff edge as Myra commanded. Lexy walked beside Nans, glancing over to see her grandmother smiling serenely, as if they were going for a walk in the park and not to their certain deaths. Either Nans had lost her marbles, or her complete lack of fear meant she had a plan to get them all out of this mess.

Lexy prayed it was the latter of the two.

"So," Nans said as they walked. "You were in on the murder all along then?"

"In on it?" Myra scowled. "I *was* it. This whole scheme is all mine. Joe has no idea. He's so clueless. All he cares about is making his stupid jewelry these days. Besides, he's too stupid and nice to come up with all this. He'd never be able to pull it off. I'm the mastermind."

"He had no idea?" Helen asked.

"None."

Myra had killed a man behind her husband's back. That kind of put Jack's secret meeting with the blonde in perspective, at least for now. Indignation rising, Lexy joined in the questioning, hoping to buy them more time. After all, she might not get another chance given how close they were to the cliff edge now. "How did you know about the coins in Ruth's car?"

Myra scoffed. "That part was easy, since I do all the bookkeeping for Joe's little hobby. He's awful with math or computers. About the only thing he *does* know how to do on the Internet is chat in his dumb coin forum. One day, he forgot to shut his screen down, and that's when I saw the post about that four-million-dollar coin. Said it was linked to an infamous heist by Nunzio Bartolli."

Ruth gasped and stumbled over a tree root, her foot slipping perilously close to the edge of the ravine. Lexy caught her arm and pulled her closer, out of harm's way.

"Don't act so shocked," Myra said, smirking. "It's not like everyone didn't know you and that gangster were shacking up together. Didn't take a rocket scientist to figure out he might've stashed those coins in that car he gave you. Stop acting like you're an innocent in all this. No way could you have lived with a man like Nunzio and not known what he was up to."

Myra waved the gun at them, urging them nearer to what looked to Lexy to be at least a fifty-foot drop down to the rocky banks of the creek below. Recent rains had swollen the waters into a rushing, treacherous torrent.

"What about Sherman Wilson?" Lexy asked, linking arms with Nans, needing her strength now more than ever. They had to find a way out of this. She had to see her Jack one more time, to find out the truth, to tell him she forgave him for whatever he'd been thinking, to tell him how much she loved him, loved their life together. How she'd never let him go without a fight. "Was killing him just a coincidence, or were you two in on this together?"

"I don't work with a partner, not where money's concerned. Joe's enough of a liability," Myra said. The cold, callous way she discussed her husband—as if he were nothing more than a piece of furniture—made Lexy treasure the special bond she and Jack shared all the more. No way would she let some blond bimbo waltz in and steal that away from her. The minute she got out of this—*if* she got out of this—she'd tell Jack how much she cared, how much she appreciated him. "Finding Sherman Wilson in the storage bay that night was just a coincidence. Unfortunately for him, we just happened to choose the same night to make our move to get that coin." She shook her head, chuckling. "Imagine my surprise when I walked into that garage and found a guy already there, pawing through the car's engine. Good thing I'd brought Joe's titanium drill to drill out the lock on the store unit and the car, since I didn't have my gun on me. Live and learn."

Ida rolled her eyes, her voice drenched in sarcasm. "How inconvenient of him."

"That's exactly what I thought too. The nerve of some people." Myra grinned. "Turns out that drill came in handy for more than just drilling out the locks that night. Of course, my first clue I wasn't alone at that storage bay should've been the missing padlock on the overhead door outside. Then again, I figured Ruth here had just had a senior moment and forgot to secure the place the last time she was there."

Ruth gave an indignant sniff. "I have never in my life been so insulted."

"I find that hard to believe." Myra shook her head. "Anyway. Yep. That drill made a nice murder weapon, if a bit too bloody for my tastes. Ruined a perfectly nice pair of Joe's white cotton archival gloves too. Those aren't cheap, you know. He says they're necessary to keep him from getting oil from his skin on those stupid, worthless coins of his, but I think some cheap old latex ones would work just fine too. Those would be a lot better if things get bloody. The cotton gloves just soaked it all in. I had a hard time getting those stains out."

"Well, it seems to me you went through an awful lot of trouble and still came up empty handed," Nans said. "You never did find the coin you wanted, did you?"

Myra advanced, and the ladies all took another step back, gravel slipping from beneath their heels to tumble down the ravine. "I'd have had more time to search if I wouldn't have had to get out of there so fast that night. Sherman Wilson should have just died quietly, like a good victim. But no. He made a huge racket before he kicked off, so I had to hightail it out of there pretty quickly to avoid being caught."

"And Joe has no idea you did any of this?" Helen asked.

"None." Myra smiled, as cold as ice. "Like I said, he's not the sharpest tack in the wall."

Lexy's heart pounded so loudly in her ears now, it nearly drowned out everything else. If Nans did have a plan to get them out of this dire situation, now would be the perfect time. Lexy peered over the cliff to see the white water swirling angrily against the jagged rocks sticking up from the river below. Yep, any time now would be marvelous.

"And it's not like Joe pays much attention to me these days, anyway. Being married awhile will do that to a couple. He's so unaware of me, he doesn't even know I've swapped out some of the most valuable coins his clients bring in for worthless ones. Honestly, I'm doing him a favor. The value vanishes once he cuts into them anyway."

"Well, that explains the argument we saw on the side-walk the other day then," Ida said, crossing her arms. "Joe seemed genuinely confused when that man accused him of switching the coins in his jewelry. Now we know why."

"Hey. We had his massive medical bills to pay," Myra said. "Plus, a girl needs to do something to maintain her appearance. Social Security only goes so far." She raised the gun to aim at Lexy again. "Speaking of which, I searched that piece of crap VW of yours the other day while it was sitting over at the body shop and didn't find that rare coin. Which means you ladies must still have it stashed somewhere." She turned the gun from Lexy to Ruth. "I'll need you to tell me where you've put it before you take your tumble over the cliff."

"I-I-" Ruth stuttered, clutching onto Helen for dear life. "I've never seen that coin. I swear."

Nans nudged Lexy slightly and gave her a wink, her gaze calm and confident as she turned to Myra and pulled a coin out of the pocket of her skirt. "Perhaps this is what you're looking for?"

Myra's eyes grew as large as saucers. "Is that—"

"Why, yes," Nans said, flicking the coin over Myra's head and into the woods behind her with a flourish of her wrist. "It is."

Myra gasped, her attention wavering from the ladies to the woods. Nans seized her opportunity. Before Lexy could react, her grandmother had rushed forward, smacking Myra upside the head with her huge beige patent-leather handbag. Ida and Helen joined in as well and, soon, Ruth too. With all those massive handbags striking her upside the head, the ladies quickly had Myra down on the ground. The gun tumbled from her hand as she used her arms to protect her head.

Sirens wailed, and Lexy picked up the gun, aiming it at Myra this time, adrenaline fizzing through her veins. They'd done it. They'd solved the case. They'd caught the killer. They'd...

Several squad cars and a black sedan pulled into the field beside the station wagon, and Jack rushed over to pull Lexy into his arms. "Are you all right? You could've gotten yourself killed, honey."

"Oh, Jack," she sobbed into his neck. "I'm sorry. I'm so sorry. I don't care about your secrets or your blonde or anything else except the fact that I love you, and I'm going to spend the rest of my life showing you just how much."

He cupped her cheeks and kissed her tenderly then rested his forehead against hers. "I think you're in shock, honey. You're not making any sense."

Lexy sniffled and pulled back slightly. "How did you find us?"

"Ida's text helped," Jack said, stepping aside as two police officers took custody of a dazed Myra. "Then we pinpointed your location using the GPS on Nans' cell phone." Jack pulled Lexy close again, kissing the top of her head. "Don't you know I'd search the ends of the earth to make sure you were safe, honey? I love you."

For the first time since this whole crazy week started, Lexy felt settled and secure. "I love you too. So, so much."

Nans walked over, interrupting their moment. "Well, I'm glad to know you listen to us *sometimes*," She fished her phone out of her enormous handbag and handed it to Jack. "Lucky thing too. After Ida passed this back to me, I left the voice recorder on. Got a full confession from Myra. All you have to do is press play."

# CHAPTER TWENTY-THREE

*T*he next day, Lexy sat at one of the small café tables outside The Cup and Cake.

Sparks of sun danced on the waterfall across the street. The smell of fresh water mingled with the scent of the extra-dark-roast coffee steaming out of her cup. The street was empty. The soft rush of the falls soothed her.

Across the street, sparrows swooped low from the branches of the nearby maple tree to snatch the crumbs left behind by the summer tourists. The mug warmed her palms as she lifted it to her lips, her taste buds welcoming the slightly bitter tang of the coffee. Everything seemed perfect and peaceful, except for her current task.

She felt closer to Jack now than she ever had, after her near brush with death. Still, she needed to get all her fears and concerns out once and for all. Talking seemed to be an issue between them lately, so the written word seemed best. Her note to her husband sat on the table before her, setting her already frazzled nerves even more on edge. She'd hoped that solving the Sherman Wilson murder case would ease the persistent tension between them, but—if anything—Jack had only been acting even more strangely since Myra's arrest. There was still something he wasn't telling her.

The phone in her pocket buzzed, and she pulled it out to see Jack's text still shining brightly on-screen. *Be home at 6pm sharp. We need to talk.*

She sighed and laid the phone on the table beside her note, staring down at the paper without really seeing it. Lexy was so distracted by all the turmoil with her husband, it took a moment for her to realize that Ruth's Oldsmobile was approaching from the end of the street.

As the vehicle neared, Lexy spotted Ruth's curly white hair barely rising above the massive dashboard, her white-gloved hands clutching the steering wheel tight at the ten and two. Ruth veered toward the curb, causing the front tire to bump up and over the barrier to stop on the sidewalk. Several nearby pedestrians scattered to avoid the oncoming car, alarmed. Thankfully, Ruth's top speed was only about five miles per hour, so it wasn't hard to get out of her way.

Lexy chuckled and slipped the letter into her pocket

as the huge boat of a car finally came to a halt in front of the bakery and the ladies got out.

Ida took a deep breath and grinned. "Nothing like solving a murder to put some pep in a gal's step."

"Yes." Nans leaned in to give Lexy a kiss on the cheek as they made their way inside the bakery. "I think we proved ourselves quite clever with this case."

"What can I get you ladies today?" Lexy followed them in and moved behind the counter. Cassie was on a break, saying she had some errands to run. "We've got some lovely caramel-swirl brownies on special and also a fresh batch of croissants still warm from the oven."

"Oh, a brownie for me, please," Helen said.

"Yes, I think I'll have one of those too, dear," Nans agreed, pulling out her wallet from her handbag. "You know, I still can't understand why that husband of yours won't listen to me more, dear. Especially when Jack knows that I'm usually right."

Laughter burst from the other ladies.

"Typical man," Ruth said, ordering a croissant for herself. "They never listen. Or admit they're wrong."

"So true." Ida chose a croissant as well, and Lexy rang them all up. Once everyone had paid, they walked back outside to sit at the table again. Ida sat across from Lexy. "Did Jack figure out how Stan the storage man was involved in all this?"

Lexy nodded. "Turns out Stan was running a chop shop out of one of his units. He had a gang of local thugs who would steal cars in the area then drive them to the storage facility. Once they got them inside the unit, the vehicles were dismantled and sold for parts. Apparently, they used a titanium drill exactly like the one Myra had of Joe's."

"Makes sense," Helen said. "Since those cut through metal. Doesn't matter if that metal is a car or a coin."

"Jack was happy too because he got to make two arrests yesterday." Lexy forced a smile. There was a time when just being with her had made Jack happy too. "After they booked in Myra at the station, he drove out to Stan's place and arrested him too. Turns out he'd lied about his alibi because he didn't want to admit he was at the facility to chop up another stolen car the night Sherman Wilson was murdered."

"Perfect!" Ruth said. "Serves that awful Stan right."

"Also true," Ida agreed.

"And we can take partial credit for helping Jack with that case as well," Nans said, sipping her tea. "Two more successes for the Ladies Detective Club."

"I have to say that was really clever of you," Lexy said to her grandmother. "Pretending you had the four-million-dollar coin and throwing it into the woods like that to distract Myra."

"Hmm." Nans gave a small smile. "I do my best, dear."

Ida swallowed her last bite of croissant, gaze narrowed. "The coin *was* fake, wasn't it?"

Nans laughed. "Of course!"

Ruth dabbed her mouth with a napkin, her bright-red lipstick barely smudged. "I do wonder whatever happened to the real coin, though. Nunzio never mentioned it to me while we were together, and now it seems to have vanished off the face of the earth."

"Eh." Nans shrugged. "I'm sure it will turn up some-day. I'm just happy we solved another case."

"No one got hurt either," Helen added. "That's always a good thing."

"True yet again." Ida stretched out her hand, and they all high-fived. "Sounds like a winner to me."

Once they'd all finished their treats, the ladies returned to Ruth's car while Lexy collected their trash and tidied up. "We need to get back to the retirement center, dear. Bingo's at three today, and Ruth and Helen both have hair appointments at the salon. See you later, and be sure to give Jack a kiss for me."

Lexy waved as the ladies drove away, then took her seat again. Her note still sat there as if mocking her. Nans and her friends were so excited and enthusiastic about solving their mysteries. It made Lexy sad to think she wouldn't be able to join them in their escapades anymore. But a promise was a promise. And as much as she loved being with the ladies, she loved Jack more. And if giving up solving cases would help save her marriage, then so be it.

Jack meant more to her than anything else.

She started writing again, putting it all down on paper—her promise not to join the ladies anymore, her commitment to their marriage, how much she loved him. All of it. Maybe this letter would show Jack how much she cared and how determined she was to save their life together.

All she could do now was hope it wasn't too little, too late.

# CHAPTER TWENTY-FOUR

*B*y the time Lexy made it home that night, her stomach was in knots. She'd been able to catch a ride with Cassie again after they'd closed at five thirty. Good thing too, since her car was still sitting in the retirement center parking lot, kaput. After what had happened with Myra, Lexy was hesitant to call for an Uber ride, and walking was out of the question. The last thing she wanted was to look like a sweaty mess when she met Jack. Things would be difficult enough as it was.

As they cruised along in Cassie's car, the air conditioning set on max, Lexy clutched the note she'd written earlier in her hand. Should she give it to Jack first and let her words explain her feelings? Or should she try to act as if everything was fine and let him start the conversation?

Her mind was still racing with these ideas when Cassie turned the corner onto Lexy's street. She frowned and peered out her window. "Isn't that Ruth's Oldsmobile?"

Cassie craned her neck to look then smiled. "Looks like it."

"What's she doing here?" Lexy frowned. Jack's instructions had been specific. Home at six, then they'd talk.

"Not sure." Cassie pulled her car over to the curb behind the Olds and cut the engine. "Let's get inside."

"Wait," Lexy said, more confused than ever. "I thought you were just dropping me off."

"Oh, well." Cassie unfastened her seat belt and opened her door. "John gave me something to give to Jack."

"I can give it to him." Lexy got out of the passenger side, her note still in her hand.

"No, I need to give it to Jack personally." Cassie tugged her toward the door. "Don't worry. It won't take long."

Lexy dug in her heels, her suspicions growing. "What's going on?"

"You'll see." Cassie opened the front door to reveal a little party inside. Everyone was there—Nans, Ruth, Ida, Helen, and even John. Sprinkles was in seventh heaven with all the extra people to give her attention and belly rubs. Jack walked over and gave Lexy a quick kiss, wrapping his arm around her waist.

"Welcome home, honey," he said. "We're celebrating."

Stunned, she blinked at her husband a moment. "Celebrating what?"

"I've got a surprise for you in the backyard." Jack winked.

"Why? It's not my birthday."

Jack took her hand and kissed her again before pulling her across the living room and down the hall. "Maybe just because I love you."

Once they'd reached the patio doors, Lexy was shocked. There, sitting just beyond the chain-link fence, in the alleyway behind their house, was a brand-new VW Bug—yellow, just like her old one. Grateful tears welled in her eyes, and she raised a shaky hand to her face. "D-Do y-you mean this is why you've been so secretive these past few weeks?"

"Of course." Jack pulled her tight against his side and kissed the top of her head. "Why else? Believe me, this was hard to keep hidden. Especially with Cassie and Nans in on it."

Lexy turned to see the rest of the party had joined them.

"Yeah," Cassie said, stifling a laugh. "I thought we

were done for when you started asking about the blonde in Jack's office. If you could've seen the look on your face..."

Pulling away from her husband, Lexy crossed her arms. "What *about* the blonde I saw in your office that day?"

"Oh, you must mean the sales lady, dear," Nans said. "She was nice enough to hand-deliver the contract to Jack that day at the station. I did my best to keep you from seeing her, but it wasn't enough, obviously."

"Why?" Jack asked, his look quizzical. "What did you think was going on?"

"I..." Note still in her hand, Lexy looked away as guilt roiled inside her. Here she was, assuming the worst of him, when the whole time, he'd been planning this wonderful surprise for her. She felt like the lowest of the low. Blinking back tears, she lowered her head. "What about all those late-night shifts you suddenly had to pull?"

"What did you think I was doing?" Jack gave her a knowing look, his honey-brown eyes sparkling with warmth and amusement. She couldn't meet his gaze as hot tears scalded her cheeks. "That woman was arranging financing for the car, honey. That's it. I swear. Then I had to visit the insurance company to get everything transferred over. The registration was the worst, though.

All those hours waiting in line at the DMV. And, of course, I had to have your new ride inspected by my mechanic too. Can't have the woman I love driving around in an unsafe vehicle." Jack laughed at the look on Lexy's face. "Did you think something was going on with the sales lady? I would never, ever look at another woman, honey. Why would I? When everything I want is already in my arms."

He sounded so sincere and earnest that her heart squeezed tight in her chest. She'd been so foolish, thinking Jack wanted to divorce her, when all he really wanted was for her to be safe and happy. Hot tears streamed down her cheeks now as she smiled through them. "Thank you, Jack. I love you too. And I intend to prove that to you for the rest of my life."

"Glad to hear it." Jack kissed her deeply then pointed to the note in her hand. "Is that for me? Can I read it?"

"What?" Lexy hurriedly crumpled her note into a ball. "Oh, no. This is nothing. A shopping list I made before I left work. That's all." She tossed it into the trash then wrapped her arms around his neck. "Kiss me again, Jack."

"Yes, ma'am." He did exactly that.

"Well, this has been a good week all around," Nans said, clearing her throat when things got a bit too heated. Lexy, cheeks hot, turned in Jack's arms to face her grandmother. "We caught two criminals. Ruth got a new love interest. And now, my dear Lexy got a new car."

Ida sighed. "Too bad we didn't find that four-million-dollar coin, though."

Lexy grinned and linked her arms through Jack's and Nans'. It *had* been a good week. The killer was caught, and she wouldn't miss her old car so much with its new identical replacement. Lexy glanced at the crumpled note in the trash. *And* now she wouldn't have to stop assisting the ladies in their investigations. "That's okay, Ida. Some things are more important than money."

**********

Sign up for my VIP reader list and get my books at the lowest discount price:
http://www.leighanndobbs.com/newsletter

Join my Facebook Readers group and get special content and the inside scoop on my books:
https://www.facebook.com/groups/ldobbsreaders

If you want to receive a text message on your cell phone for new releases, text COZYMYSTERY to 88202 (sorry, this only works for US cell phones!)

No Scone Unturned

-------

Mooseamuck Island Cozy Mystery Series

\* \* \*

A Zen For Murder

A Crabby Killer

A Treacherous Treasure

-------

Mystic Notch

Cat Cozy Mystery Series

\* \* \*

Ghostly Paws

A Spirited Tail

A Mew To A Kill

Paws and Effect

Probable Paws

-------

Silver Hollow

Paranormal Cozy Mystery Series

***

A Spell of Trouble (Book 1)

Spell Disaster (Book 2)

Nothing to Croak About (Book 3)

*Cry Wolf* (Book 4)

-------

*Blackmoore Sisters*

*Cozy Mystery Series*

\* \* \*

*Dead Wrong*

*Dead & Buried*

*Dead Tide*

*Buried Secrets*

*Deadly Intentions*

*A Grave Mistake*

*Spell Found*

*Fatal Fortune*

-------

**Magical Romance with a Touch of Mystery**

***

*Something Magical*

*Curiously Enchanted*

## Romantic Comedy

***

## Corporate Chaos Series

*In Over Her Head (book 1)*

-------

## Contemporary Romance

***

*Reluctant Romance*

-------

## Sweet Romance (Written As Annie Dobbs)

*Hometown Hearts Series*

***

No Getting Over You (Book 1)

--------

***

## Sweetrock Sweet and Spicy Cowboy Romance

*Some Like It Hot*

*Too Close For Comfort*

----

## Regency Romance

\* \* \*

## Scandals and Spies Series:

*Kissing The Enemy*

*Deceiving the Duke*

*Tempting the Rival*

*Charming the Spy*

*Pursuing the Traitor*

## The Unexpected Series:

*An Unexpected Proposal*

*An Unexpected Passion*

## Dobbs Fancytales:

Dobbs Fancytales Boxed Set Collection

———

## Western Historical Romance

\*\*\*

## Goldwater Creek Mail Order Brides:

*Faith*

## American Mail Order Brides Series:

Chevonne: Bride of Oklahoma

——————————————

## Lexy's Cream Puff Recipe

### Ingredients:

- 1/2 cup butter, cut up
- 1 cup water
- 1/2 teaspoon salt
- 1 cup all purpose flour
- 5 eggs
- 2 cups whipping cream, chilled
- 1 1/2 teaspoons pure vanilla extract
- 1/4 cup confectioners' sugar
- 1/2 teaspoon cream of tartar

## Directions:
### To make the puffs:

- Preheat oven to 400 degrees (f).
- Mix butter, salt, and water in a medium-sized saucepan and heat on medium-high until it boils. Stir in the flour. Keep stirring until it forms into a smooth ball. Remove from heat. Let cool for 5 minutes.
- Add 4 of the eggs, one at a time, to the flour mixture, stirring constantly to make sure each egg is mixed in before you add the next.
- Continue beating dough mixture until it is smooth and shiny.
- Grease a cookie sheet, or line with parchment.
- You can make the "puffs" two ways. Lexy uses a pastry bag with a 5/8" tip to pipe the dough into rounds. But she's a professional—the easier way with less to clean up is simply drop 1/4 cup of dough onto the cookie sheet.
- Whisk the remaining egg with 1 tablespoon of water and brush over the top of the puffs.

- Bake until puffs rise and are golden brown— about 30 minutes.
- Cut a split in each puff for steam to escape and cool on a wire rack.

## To make the cream:

- Chill the bowl and beaters.
- Whip the cream on this highest setting until it begins to thicken.
- Add the sugar evenly while still beating.
- Add the cream of tartar evenly while still beating.
- Add the vanilla.
- Continue to beat until stiff peaks form.

## Assemble the cream puff:

Cut open the puffs and discard any doughy insides then fill with the cream. Enjoy!

# ABOUT THE AUTHOR

USA Today Bestselling author Leighann Dobbs has had a passion for reading since she was old enough to hold a book, but she didn't put pen to paper until much later in life. After a twenty-year career as a software engineer with a few side trips into selling antiques and making jewelry, she realized you can't make a living reading books, so she tried her hand at writing them and discovered she had a passion for that, too! She lives in New Hampshire with her husband, Bruce, their trusty Chihuahua mix, Mojo, and beautiful rescue cat, Kitty.

Her book "Dead Wrong" won the "Best Mystery Romance" award at the 2014 Indie Romance Convention.

Her book "Ghostly Paws" was the 2015 Chanticleer Mystery & Mayhem First Place category winner in the Animal Mystery category.

Don't miss out on the early buyers discount on

Leighann's next cozy mystery - signup for email notifications:

http://www.leighanndobbs.com/newsletter


Want text alerts for new releases? TEXT alert straight on your cellphone. Just text COZYMYSTERY to 88202 (sorry, this only works for US cell phones!)


Connect with Leighann on Facebook:

http://facebook.com/leighanndobbsbooks


Join her VIP Readers group on Facebook:

https://www.facebook.com/groups/ldobbsreaders